Lock Down Publications and Ca$h
Presents

I0666785

HUB CITY MENACE 3

A Sister's Code

Written By
J. WHITE

Copyright © 2025 J. WHITE
HUB CITY MENACE 3

All rights reserved. No part of this book may be reproduced in any form or by electronic or mechanical means, including information storage and retrieval systems without permission in writing from the publisher, except by a reviewer who may quote brief passages in review.

First Edition 2025

Printed in the United States of America

This is a work of fiction. Names, characters, places, and incidents either are products of the author's imagination or are used fictitiously. Any similarity to actual events or locales or persons, living or dead, is entirely coincidental.

Lock Down Publications
P.O. Box 944
Stockbridge, GA 30281
www.lockdownpublications.com

Like our page on Facebook: Lock Down Publications
www.facebook.com/lockdownpublications.ldp

Stay Connected with Us!

Text **LOCKDOWN** to 22828 to stay up-to-date with new releases, sneak peaks, contests and more…

Like our page on Facebook:
Lock Down Publications

Join Lock Down Publications/The New Era Reading Group

Visit our website:
www.lockdownpublications.com

Follow us on Instagram:
Lock Down Publications

Email Us: We want to hear from you!

PART I

"When It All Falls Down"

Chapter 1
Press The Button

"How could—?... Wait a—I thought... Derrick?" Mecia stammered. Her eyes still watered, the tears were not to be held back. They were inevitable. There, standing before her was her baby brother live in the flesh. The same brother she said she never wanted to see again. The one she blamed and held accountable for the death of their grandparents. Surprisingly, Mecia rushed over to Big D and embraced his large form as the flood gates opened behind her pupils. "Oh, brother... I- I'm sorry—" she tried to speak, holding back gut-wrenching sobs.

"Shh," Big D soothed his sister, rubbing her back comfortingly as he held her tight to his chest, his chin resting softly on her head of unkempt hair. "It's gone be okay. I'm here now."

"I should have never treated you like that." Mecia squeezed harder "You never even got to meet him." The waves of emotions were hitting pretty hard.

"Mec, it's alright. Trust me. I ain't mad at you. It was all my fault. Everything that happened back then." Derrick was saying as he lifted his chin and began to reminisce a bit in his mind. "I was out of control at that point in time, so I get it. It does hurt that I never met Marcus but he's my nephew, my family and I love him the same," D spoke from the heart.

"My baby boy is gone..." Mecia cried.

"Look at me sis," Big D said to Mecia lifting her head and wiping her soaked cheeks with a large thumb. "Marcus may not be right in here with us," he said giving the room a glance. "But he will forever be right here," he clarified with his index finger pointed toward her heart. "We gonna figure this shit out, don't worry."

In that instant, all the harbored ill feelings and disdain Mecia once held for her baby brother was gone. Deep down she knew she couldn't hold that grudge anymore. She had forgiven him for the death of their grandparents and even spoke some to him throughout his incarceration, but seeing him again was just different. Despite their rocky past, she knew that she needed him. Especially now, the whole family did. Mecia squeezed him harder and wept softly. "But they killed my baby." Her heart hurt every time she said those words or even thought about it.

"And I killed them," Big D stated boldly and without regret as he held her in his arms.

Before Mecia completely understood his words well enough to form a response, Kam's scream interrupted. "Oh my God… Look!" She hurried to raise the volume.

BREAKING NEWS: *"This just in, we have multiple reports on some sort of bombing and or explosion tonight in the downtown Lubbock area. Here's investigative reporter Gabrielle Renee'with more details, Gabrielle…"*

"Thanks Jack. Yes, I'm here at the scene downtown on Main St. where it's clear there has been a terrible tragedy suffered tonight. Reports began to flood in about less than hour ago when the 1st precinct of Lubbock was targeted in what is believed to be an intentional terrorist attack. As you can see behind me is a solid half mile of raging orange flames the fire department are still fighting to maintain and put out. The nature and reasoning for this attack is still unknown but there have already been whispers that this could be possible backlash from a recent police shooting of

another young African American city resident or possibly have some connection with the Murder of Police Officer Brian Todd, though no direct correlations have been proven at this time. Further reports at this moment are saying it's believed the city of Lubbock may have just lost almost fifty percent of its Law Enforcement Officers and resources in this devastating attack as this blaze continues. It is a sad day as we all witness the aftermath occurring real time. My sources are now saying a few minutes prior to the bombing attack all the power within the precinct and surrounding area buildings were cut along with all channels of communication, both outgoing and incoming were knocked out somehow. This is certainly unlike anything the city has ever seen or experienced before. Exactly how and why this tragic event has taken place remains unclear but I can assure you this investigation will remain a top priority and the second we have more of an understanding here we will be back with an update-"

Mecia, her eyes still wet with tears, turned to the television, a strange mix of horror and understanding washing over her face. As the newscaster detailed the catastrophic attack on the police precinct, Big D, sensing her distress, began to speak.

"I know this might not be the easiest thing to understand," he started, his voice heavy with guilt, "But I had to do what I did. I couldn't let them get away with what they did to Marcus."

To his surprise, Mecia didn't react with anger or condemnation. Instead, a serene smile spread across her face. "You did the right thing, Derrick," she said softly. "You avenged Marcus."

A sigh of relief passed over Big D as he realized the depth of his sister's understanding. He pulled her into a tight embrace, their shared grief and newfound resolve binding them closer than ever before.

Breaking the embrace, Mecia turned to her daughters, Kam and Ke'. "Girls, I think it's time you properly met your Uncle Derrick."

Kam, still reeling from the shock of the news, stepped forward, her eyes wide with a mix of fear and awe. She embraced her uncle hesitantly, her body language betraying her underlying emotions. Ke, ever the observant one, followed suit, her small arms wrapping around her uncle's waist.

Big D, feeling a surge of familial love, pulled his nieces closer. "I'm here now, ladies," he assured them, his voice gentle. "I'll protect you."

As the four stood together, a sense of unity and purpose filled the room. They had weathered a storm, and now, they faced the future, stronger and more determined than ever.

The tension in the room began to dissipate as the initial shock of the news wore off. Big D, now settled on the couch, spent the next few moments getting to know his nieces better. He asked about their interests, their dreams, and their lives. Kam and Ke' initially shy, gradually warmed up to him, sharing stories and bittersweet moments of laughter.

Jax, still holding his mother close, offered silent comfort. Words couldn't help much at the moment. I mean nothing he said would bring Marcus back. His heart ached for her loss, but he knew that his presence was a source of strength. He stroked her hair gently, expressions of reassurance.

Mecia, feeling a sense of peace she hadn't experienced in a long time, smiled at the sight of her family. She was grateful for their love and support. She knew that standing together, coupled with the grace of God they could overcome any challenge. Even one such tragedy as this.

As the night wore on, a slight sense of normalcy settled over the household. The reality of the everything was still hard to fully accept, but it was tempered by the warmth of family and the hopes of a brighter future together and maybe, in time some explanation and understanding.

Mecia, being the caretaker she was, tried to lighten the mood and suggested, "Maybe I should cook something. I don't have much of an appetite but none of us have eaten in ages and probably should."

Big D chuckled lightly, rubbing his large stomach. "Well, I could definitely eat something."

His simple playful remark brought a much-needed laugh to the room. Kam, however, had a different idea. "No, mama, you need to rest. It's late, you've been through more than anyone should have to handle.

I can just grab us something to eat real quick. Any ideas on what I should get?"

Big D paused, considering the options. Then, with a blinding grin, he said, "Surprise us."

Kam nodded, understanding the assignment. "Okay, I'll be back soon."

Ke' rose from the couch, eager to join her sister. "Want me to go with you?" she asked hopefully.

Kam declined. "No, it's okay, sis. You stay here with Uncle Derrick and keep mama company. I'll just run to Mickey D's. I'll call when I get there to see what everyone wants."

With that said, Kam grabbed her keys from the key holder on the wall and headed out the door. A few steps later, she made it to her car, got in and just paused in thought for a second. Her mind flashed to Marcus and how much she missed him already. She connected her phone via Bluetooth to the speakers and began to play the instrumental of a new track she was working on with Stephen for Marcus and just sang her heart out.

Life was hitting hard and she was doing her best to stay sane and strong. As she backed out of the driveway, unease settled over the group in the house. No one knew that would be the last time they would see Kam alive. The simple act of running to the nearby fast-food joint would turn into a tragedy. A victim in deliberate attack that would shatter their world into pieces no family could repair.

***

Lost in the rhythm of her unfinished track, Kam drove slowly down the silent street. Her mind a tangle of raw emotions, each note a reflection of the pain and longing she felt in her soul. Unbeknownst to her, a sinister plot was unfolding just a few houses away.

Terry, Tory, and Bundle were parked in the shadows, their eyes fixed on Mecia's house. They spotted Kam the second she stepped out.

***

Tory's incessant questioning about Bundle's past and present endeavors irritated Terry, but he maintained his focus on the target and goal at hand.

"Damn, y'all lovebirds really gone sit up here and play 21 Questions or what?" Terry muttered, his voice laced with impatience.

Tory, unfazed, playfully retorted. "Yeah, nigga, 21 Questions! Shit, maybe 22. I'm bored back here. Absolutely no action," she pouted, her eyes scanning the street. Bundle chuckled, his nervous energy vibrating through him.

"Well, save some of that shit for y'all's first date or something," Terry joked, trying to lighten the mood. He laughed, a deep, hearty sound that echoed in the confined space.

Tory blushed, a rare display of vulnerability. To cover her embarrassment, she shifted her attention to the glowing detonator in her hand.

"Fuck all that, when do I get to push this button?" She asked, her voice filled with anticipation and seriousness.

Terry paused, his gaze unwavering. "Shit, a lot sooner than you think. Here that bitch, come now!" He replied, a disturbing grin spreading across his face.

***

Kam belted out note after note, her voice the cry of angels. Relief washed over her momentarily while she sang, replacing the ache of loss. She was almost to the end of the block approaching the red stop sign at the intersection marking the turn onto the main street. As she lifted her foot from the gas pedal, preparing to slow down, she had no clue the world around her was about to erupt in a blinding flash of white-hot fire.

***

Back in the Red Caprice, the tension and anticipation rose. Terry, his eyes glued to Kam's car slammed his fist on the dashboard with. "Damn that bitch! Press the button sis."

"Hold on, hold on! We can't blow her up just yet!" Bundle interjected.

Terry and Tory whipped their heads towards him, confusion etched on their faces. "What the hell are you talking about?" Terry barked.

"C4, nigga." Bundle explained, his voice barely a whisper. "We put four charges on that car. If she's too close, within our radius with all of these cars lined up and down the street, if she goes boom, we all go boom!"

A beat of stunned silence followed. Terry cursed under his breath. "Why you ain't been said that?"

"Shit I thought that was self-explanatory," Bundle retorted, his voice laced with a hint of defiance.

Terry glared at him, but the urgency of the situation eclipsed his anger. "Alright, alright," he conceded, rubbing his temples with a sigh. "So how far does the bitch gotta be?"

Bundle squinted through the windshield, calculating the distance. "Another hundred and fifty feet, maybe two hundred. Just gotta get her a little further down the block, closer to the stop sign."

The seconds stretched into an eternity. Bundle raised his hand dramatically, mimicking a countdown. Sweat beaded on Tory's forehead as she locked eyes with him in the rearview mirror.

"Five... four... three..." Bundle's voice was a low growl.

Tory's heart pounded like a drum solo in her chest. Two... one...

With a trembling hand, she slammed her palm down on the detonator.

***

In Kam's car, the world became a cacophony of sound, fire and fury. The deafening roar of the explosion drowned out the final notes of her beautiful song.

A searing inferno engulfed her, the heat an unbearable torment. In the blink of an eye, she was hurtling through the air, now a mangled marionette ripped from the strings of life.

The last image that registered in her mind was a blinding white light, followed by the chilling certainty that she was joining Marcus beyond the veil.

Chapter 2
Shattered Peace

The blackened night sky was now lit with vibrant orange flames outside. The devastating explosion echoed through the neighborhood, shattering the fragile peace that had grown within Mecia's home. Jax, his senses on high alert, bolted towards the front door, Big D close behind him.

Ke', too scared to explore and grasp the full act horror unfolding, she just clung to her mother in the living room. Mecia, however, felt the earth shift beneath her feet. A primal scream tore from her throat, a mother's intuition recognizing the impossible in a heartbeat. "Stay here," Jax yelled to his mother and sister. As he flung open the door, the blast furnace of heat attacked him. The overwhelming smell of burning rubber, metal and flesh filled his nostrils, a sickening aroma of destruction. Big D, followed suit. Together, they sprinted towards the source of the soul-crushing sound -the intersection.

The scene that greeted them was a nightmare made real. Kam's Range Rover, once a symbol of her independence, was reduced to mangled shreds of luxury, engulfed in flames that cast an ominous glow. Hot twisted metal, now littered the street, a testament to the raw power of the blast.

A wave of nausea hit Big D as he spotted a lone sneaker, charred and smoking, lying several feet away in the road. It was unmistakably Kam's. The despair was a physical weight, pressing down on his chest, threatening to suffocate him.

Suddenly, a screech of tires pierced the air. From the opposite end of the street, a dark car sped away, its tail lights momentarily cutting through the smoke and fire catching D's attention. This fleeting glimpse sent a jolt of rage through Big D. This wasn't just some random accident. Someone – had just done this!

Jax, hurt and confused, his face streaked with tears and soot, screamed Kam's name in vain, his voice swallowed by the inferno. The ground beneath his feet vibrated with the frantic pounding of his own heart. Big D pulled him back, a fierce protectiveness surging through him. They couldn't get any closer, not with the flames still raging. But their eyes never left the burning wreckage, a silent prayer escaping their lips.

Off in the distance, the wail of sirens grew louder...closer.

Firetrucks and police cars converging in on the scene, their flashing lights turning the night into a surreal light show. Within minutes, the firefighters would be battling the blaze, while paramedics assessed the damage caused by the explosion to any who may have been hurt.

News of the explosion spread like wildfire throughout the neighborhood. People spilled out of their homes, their faces etched with shock and horror. Some distraught and in disbelief. Whispers of yet another terrorist attack filled the air, adding to the rapidly growing panic in the city. Jax and Big D just stood there, numb with grief, the heat of the inferno radiating off the asphalt, mirroring the pain that consumed them.

Without being noticed right away, Mecia stumbled out of the house towards them, quiet, trembling, her eyes reflecting the inferno's malevolent glow. As soon as she spotted the wreckage, she began to lose it. "Kam..." she whispered, her voice barely audible, a single tear tracing a path down her dust-streaked cheek. "Oh, Lord why. NO! NO! Please NO!"

Mecia got weak at the knees and was about to fall down before Big D pulled her into a crushing embrace, the silent promise to find her daughter's killer hanging heavy in the smoke. The flames roar, revealing the horrific truth, their world as they knew it was under siege, and what made everything so scary was the fact nobody knew why. The peace they craved had been replaced by a burning desire for justice – justice they would be determined to get themselves, no matter the cost.

The sirens wailed, their insistent cry cutting too close for comfort. Big D's demeanor shifted, his grip on Mecia lessened and his eyes widened. A hint of fear replacing the hardened resolve in his eyes. He knew he couldn't stay. As much as it tore at his soul, he had to leave his family behind in that moment in order to be there for them in the future. The encroaching danger was too great, the risk too high for a man of his level of infamy who was supposed to be dead.

Jax heard the sirens as well and turned to Big D. "Unc, you gotta go man. Get out of here now!"

D was silent but attentive. He understood. Reluctantly, he fully released Mecia turned and strode towards the black hearse, its sleek silhouette a stark contrast against the smoky backdrop on the block. The hearses engine roared to life, a guttural growl that seemed to echo his own internal turmoil. He slipped behind the wheel, the leather cool beneath his touch.

As he pulled away from the curb, he glanced back one last time at his family in the rearview, a silent prayer for those he was leaving behind. The smoke billowed, obscuring the scene, a fitting metaphor for the uncertainty that now clouded his future.

With a heavy foot on the accelerator, he plunged the hearse into the chaotic traffic. The city was beginning to feel like a warzone, cars careening wildly, people fleeing in panic. His destination was unclear, a blank void in the future. All he knew was that he had to escape this situation and find safety. He needed to survive at all costs. The road ahead was fraught with much danger and uncertainty.

Chapter 3
Just The Three Of Us

Tina's garage door creaked open. Big D, his heart hammering against his ribs like a caged animal, stepped into the dimly lit house. He was moving cautiously with stealth in the silence of the home. The scent of woodsmoke coming from the fireplace and something faintly floral overtook him, a strange juxtaposition that mirrored the chaos swirling within him.

He expected to find Tina somewhere upstairs, her face etched with worry from not hearing from him yet following his daring escape. Instead, the sight that met him was nothing short of astonishing.

Turning to the living room, he saw Tina sat on the couch, a special glint in her eyes, a glass of amber liquid clutched in her hand. But beside her, nestled against the cushions, was Angela, her hand resting possessively on Tina's thigh.

Yes, Angela!

His same fiery, independent, strong-willed lover of the past decade Angela, who he'd always imagined would rather wrestle a bear than share him. Her role in his regained freedom was so pivotal at that moment nothing but guilt consumed him.

A stunned silence filled the room. Big D blinked, unsure if he was hallucinating. The dim lamplight cast a long, dancing shadow across the room, making the scene appear surreal, almost dreamlike. Angela, noticing his bewildered expression, finally broke the silence.

"Welcome home, D," she said, her voice a low purr, a hint of steel underlying the seductive tone. "We've been waiting for you."

Tina added. "As you can see, me and Angela have had a little... discussion, while you were away."

Discussion? That was an understatement. It had been a brutal dance of power, a game of chess played out in the dark. Both women, driven by an unwavering loyalty to D, had discovered each other's existence during his incarceration.

Instead of the expected catfight and fallout with D, an unexpected understanding had blossomed; a fragile truce forged in the mix of their shared obsession.

They'd spent countless hours on the phone, initially fueled by anger and resentment of one another. But as they delved deeper, they discovered a shared vulnerability, a profound love for the same man, and a chilling realization that they were more alike than they dared to admit. Both were survivors, both had played their own dangerous games, both knew the price of freedom.

And so, the two beautiful women made a pact, an agreement born from necessity. They would not choose sides, not in the traditional sense. They would build a bond, based on the strength of their shared love for D. They would become a force, a formidable trio, capable of navigating the treacherous waters that lay ahead.

It was simple, they would keep their unconventional arrangement a secret until D returned, whenever that day came. They would let him bask in the illusion of normalcy, of being reunited with the women he loved. Only then would they reveal the truth, the truth that might shock him, might confuse him, or might even enrage him at first. But they knew, with certainty, that he would ultimately submit.

Now, as D stood frozen in the doorway, the weight of their unspoken agreement hung heavily in the air. The silence stretched, punctuated only by the ticking of the grandfather clock in the hallway, a metronome counting down the seconds. Finally, D found his voice, his words tumbling out in a rush.

"What... what is this?"

Tina and Angela exchanged a knowing glance. This was the moment of truth. As the initial shock began to subside, a flicker of amusement, dark and predatory, danced in Big D's eyes. He couldn't help but chuckle, a low, rumbling sound that echoed through the room. It was a laugh of disbelief.

He glanced at Tina and Angela, their expressions a mix of amusement and a chilling sense of anticipation. He could see the unspoken question in their eyes: What's so funny?

But Big D didn't answer. Instead, he let his laughter linger in the air, a silent acknowledgment of the absurdity of the situation. He was still reeling from the revelation, still grappling with the emotions that swirled within him – fear, anger, and a strange, unsettling sense of excitement. But for a brief moment, he found solace in the shared humor, a reminder that life, even in its most unexpected twists and turns, could still hold moments of dark, twisted amusement.

Chapter 4
The Unknown

The laughter died down, replaced by a suffocating silence. Big D's gaze drifted towards the charred remains of Leslie's house across the street, a stark reminder of the harsh realities that lurked beyond the walls of his home. He stared at the smoldering ruins, his mind a whirlwind of conflicting emotions.

Guilt gnawed at him, a relentless beast. He blamed himself for his niece and nephew's death. For all the chaos that had descended upon his family. He had thought he was protecting them, that he was making things right. Instead, he had brought the war to their doorstep.

And now, Leslie, his old friend and business partner, was gone. Another casualty. Perhaps not directly tied into everything he had going on but the timing couldn't have been worse. Anger clawed its way to the surface, threatening to erupt. He just couldn't understand who was doing all this? What did they want?

And why?

He couldn't understand it. And a man of his pedigree always understood.

"What happened over there?" He finally asked Tina, his voice a hoarse croak, the words catching in his throat. His eyes, filled with a mixture of grief and a chilling sense of dread, met hers.

Tina's smile vanished, replaced by a look of profound grief. Her eyes, usually sparkling, were now dull and lifeless, reflecting the charred remains of the house across the street. "Leslie... she didn't make it, D."

The news hit him like a physical blow, a searing pain exploding in his chest. Leslie, his friend, his business partner, gone. "How exactly? What happened?" He demanded, his voice rising, a desperate edge creeping into his tone. The anger that had been simmering beneath the surface erupted, a ferocious beast unleashed.

Tina hesitated, her eyes darting towards Angela, seeking unspoken confirmation. "It was... it was a fire. A terrible fire. They saying it was an accidental death. They believe she was maybe smoking while in bed and caught some sheets on fire but… I know what I saw beforehand and after the fact. "And that's some bullshit…" she trailed off, her voice trembling, the words catching in her throat. "Those kids had something to do with it."

"What kids?" Big D demanded, his fists clenched so tightly his knuckles turned white. "Who would do something like that out the blue?" He shook his head trying to clear it. "Man all this is too much. My nephew and my niece are dead—"

Angela and Tina cut him off immediately. They knew about everything that happened all the way up to the tragedy with Marcus but hadn't heard anything about one of Big D's nieces. "What do you mean your niece is dead?" Angela asked stepping closer.

When D brought them up to speed, their hearts broke a little more. Fear, cold and sharp, pierced through them, a frigid tendril snaking its way through their veins. The chilling way he spoke of violence as if it were merely a game, something they should be growing use to.

He looked at Tina and Angela, their faces etched with worry. They were scared, he could see it. Their fear was a tangible presence in the room. But they were also strong, resilient and unwilling to just sit idle.

Chapter 5
Echoes Of Violence

Back in front of Mecia's house, the block was a scene of horror, a grotesque parody of its former tranquility. Dust motes danced in the beams of the few street lights that still worked, illuminating the debris-strewn wreckage. Some vehicles close in proximity and other homes were now a twisted and mangled wreck, yard furniture overturned; lawns reduced to charred fragments. And at the center of it all, a cringe worthy scene of death.

Kam's Pink Range Rover, once a symbol of her independence and success, was now a sad sight to see, its ruined remains a constant reminder to the devastating power of the blast. The sight was so gruesome, so utterly heartbreaking, that even some detectives averted their gaze, their stomachs churning in silent protest.

The arrival of the police brought a fresh wave of chaos. Officers, their faces accusatory, their eyes hardened by years of witnessing the worst humanity had to offer, cordoned off the area, pushing back the throng of onlookers. News crews were like vultures circling a carcass, jostling for position, their cameras flashing, desperate to capture the unfolding tragedy for the morbid consumption of the masses.

Detective Crockerette ducked under yellow caution tape, his face a mask of grit and determination, as he pushed his way through the crowd. He was a towering figure, his dark skin high in contrast against the pale faces of the other fellow officers. Crockerette was a rarity in the LPD, a lone wolf in a pack of sheep, one of only three Black detectives on the force. He had a reputation for his unwavering integrity, a reputation built on a foundation of shattered dreams and a relentless pursuit of justice.

He had been assigned to this case, an uncanny twist of fate considering his previous involvement with the family. He was the lead detective on the case of Marcus Cook, Kam's younger brother, who had been killed in a controversial police shooting. Crockerette had also been investigating the homicide Marcus was suspected of committing before his death, a case that had left a bitter taste in his mouth, a gnawing sense of injustice that had never truly subsided.

Now, he found himself back in the Cook family's lives, this time investigating the possible brutal murder of their beloved daughter, another hometown hero and one of America's most influential musical icons.

Finding Jax and Mecia standing in front of their home seemingly lost in the midst of everything around them, he stepped to them with caution.

"Ms. Cook," Crockerette said, his voice a low rumble, approaching the distraught mother. "I'm so sorry for your loss."

Mecia, a ball of grief and rage, barely acknowledged him, her focus mainly on the many people surrounding their property gawking for footage and answers. "Get them out of here!" She growled, her voice raw with pain, gesturing towards the news crews. "This is a private matter."

Crockerette understood. This was a family in mourning, their lives shattered by a senseless act of violence. But he also knew that every piece of evidence, every witness statement, was crucial.

"Ms. Cook, I understand," Crockerette said, his voice soothing, though the sympathy in his eyes was a thin veneer. "But I need to understand what happened here tonight. Was there any indication that this was a targeted attack? Any threats to your family. Any enemies?"

Mecia, her eyes fixed on the remnants of her daughter's car, couldn't speak. The words caught in her throat, a sob escaping her lips. Tears streamed down her face, blurring the already horrifying scene before her.

Jax, who had been standing silent watching the scene unfold with a growing sense of dread, stepped forward, furious. "What the hell do you think you're doing?" He snarled, his voice low and menacing. "You cops are vultures, circling and picking at the bones. You don't care about justice, you care about headlines! What the fuck else do y'all want from us? Do you think if we knew what was going on or why we would have let this happen? This shit is crazy man, and we are just as lost as you are!"

Crockerette, unfazed by Jax's anger, simply regarded him with a steely gaze. "Calm down, son. I'm just trying to do my job."

"Your job?" Jax scoffed, his voice dripping with sarcasm. "Your job is to protect and serve, right? Well, you've done a damn poor job of that lately."

Crockerette's eyes narrowed. He sensed a volatile undercurrent beneath Jax's anger, something more than just grief. "Look, I understand you're upset, who wouldn't be given the circumstances," Crockerette said calmly. "But I need answers. Now I know that this may be a lot to handle but bear with me."

Mecia still sobbed, getting more uncontrollable by the minute. She just stared at the man as he carried on. "Ma'am I hate to be the bearer of such bad news, especially given the circumstances in which your family is currently facing.

In no way am I trying to add insult to injury, but have you been contacted about the death of your brother Derrick Cook? I have it on good word he was pronounced dead at the federal facility where he was incarcerated, less than 48 hours ago."

Knowing the exact situation with her brother already didn't lessen the blow as he delivered it. Mecia hurt as if she had just reunited with him. Hearing this officer claim he was dead, losing two children the way she had and battling a severe heart condition daily, it was all just too much. She remained silent and unresponsive.

Jax saw this and cut in. "As you can see officer, we don't know nothin'. Now I gotta get my moms away from here."

"What you can do is get your mother inside. We'll give her some time to recoup. But I need to speak with you privately now," the Detective said, leaving no room for further protest.

Jax hesitated, his gaze drifting to his mother, her shoulders slumped, her body trembling. He knew he needed to get her some space from these people.

"Fine," Jax conceded, his voice still laced with anger. "But let's make it quick."

Crockerette nodded and led Jax away from the crowd when he returned, towards a relatively quiet area not too far from where he parked. As they walked, Crockerette casually adjusted his jacket, revealing the view of his left arm entirely.

On his ring finger, a small, intricate tattoo caught the light – two stylized interlocking 'C's, almost imperceptible to the untrained eye.

Jax, his attention momentarily diverted, noticed the tattoo. Something about it resonated deep within him and triggered a dark recognition. He knew those symbols. They belonged to the Corona Cartel, headed by no one other than Christo.

Crockerette, sensing Jax's sudden shift in attention, turned to face him, a thin smirk spreading across his lips. "You know what this means, don't you, Jax?"

Jax felt a wave of nausea wash over him. He knew what those symbols represented. He was in business with Christo.

He had been a valuable asset, a conduit between the streets and the higher echelons of the criminal underworld.

But lately, things had gotten… complicated making it difficult for Jax to fulfill his complete obligations to this organization. The heat was on. His family dying, his child missing. And now, this.

"I think I do," Jax replied, his voice a low growl. "What you tryna say, Detective?"

Crockerette chuckled, a low, unsettling sound. "It means," hc said, his voice dropping to a conspiratorial whisper, "That we're more alike than you might think. Much more alike. And we could have some really big problems. We have to talk. I need to know everything you know."

Jax's mouth said nothing but the curiosity in his eyes said everything.

A silent beat passed. He was having some serious complications with this entire ordeal. On one hand he thought to himself, *"Damn am I a snitch if I talk to this cop or is it okay because he is supposed to be one of us…What do I do? My Brother, My Sister, My Business…"*

Then, Detective Crockette made a statement and began to ask questions that begin to change the dynamic of everything. "Kid, let's cut to the chase you know exactly what this means," he raised his tattooed finger. "I know about your ties to this organization, and that's the second reason I'm here. We are on the same team."

Listen Jax, I understand you may be feeling some conflict about this and I don't blame you. But the bottom line is we are both going to be in hot water soon if I don't get some answers. Let's face the facts and I don't mean to sound like an asshole here," the Detective mocked raised his hands, "But look at this madness." He pointed towards the obliterated car and debris. "This is nothing compared to the wrath the Corona Cartel will enforce if business doesn't get back up and running smoothly. In the last month, things here in the city have gone from bad to worse. At first it was easy to look over and most things could have been considered a coincidence and just very unfortunate, but upon further inspection it's no doubt that you and your family are somehow tied to the center of it all. Starting with the murders Byron Parker and DeMarco Lee. Moving on to your younger brother and sister both killed in a way other than natural. Reports of your Uncle Derrick Cook untimely and strange passing. There is just too much going on here. The head of the Cartel wants answers and for everything to stop, now. Or we both know this game goes when orders are defied. So Jax tell me what you know about all these cases and how it involves you and is affecting our business. I hope you understand both are lives dependent on it… So, what can you tell me?"

Chapter 6
The Morning After

The rising morning sun was a sickly yellow eye peering through the grimy windowpane. Big D lay motionless, his gaze fixed on the ceiling mirror, his mind full of conflicting emotions at the moment as he looked at three nude reflections. Beneath him, Tina and Angela both naked slept peacefully, their soft breaths a rhythmic counterpoint to the city sounds that filtered through the open window. The distant wails of sirens became a new soundtrack to the city's descent into chaos.

Tina was curled into his side, her arm draped lazily over his chest. Angela laying on the opposite side, her thick legs intertwined with his, a contented sigh escaping her lips. The night before had been a kaleidoscope of emotions, both good and bad. Then a sensual journey that had been both exhilarating and deeply pleasing. Yet, the afterglow had quickly faded, replaced by a cold dread that seeped into his bones.

The news of all these deaths, the weight of the unknown – these events overshadowing his newfound happiness with his freedom and connection with the women he loved. Things were crumbling around him, a once thriving city was now a breeding ground for fear and despair. He, along with the women he loved and his family now caught in the crossfire, all pawns in a game they barely understood the rules to and definitely didn't know all the players.

He thought of the charred remains of Leslie's house, of the worry gripped the city in the wake of the recent violence everywhere. He thought of his own vulnerability, of the enemies he had made in his lifetime, both known and unknown. A shiver ran down his spine, a premonition of impending doom. He felt like a sitting duck, a prize to be claimed by whoever emerged victorious from this war.

A small groan escaped Tina's lips, and she shifted closer, nuzzling her face against his chest. "Morning, sleepyhead," she murmured, her voice drowsy.

Big D turned his head, a forced smile gracing his lips. "Morning, beautiful." He glanced at Angela, who stirred beside him, a contented purr rumbling in her chest. He leaned down and kissed them both, savoring the warmth of their skin against his. But even as he did, a wave of worry washed over him, cold and insidious. The sweetness of the moment was fleeting, a fragile oasis in a storm-tossed sea. He knew that the calm before the storm was often the most deceptive. And he knew, with a chilling certainty, that the storm was upon them.

When Tina flipped on the TV and the breaking news broadcast flashed across the screen, the blood drained from his face. The images were horrific – the city in flames, buildings collapsing, people screaming in terror. It was a descent into a living nightmare, a stark reminder of the fragile nature of life and the brutality of the world they now inhabited.

***

The air in the living room, now heavy with the scent of burnt cannabis, and was thick with unspoken dread. Jax sat on the edge of the plastic-wrapped sofa, motionless. The sleek chrome of the pistol in his hand glinted menacingly in the dim light filtering through the cracks in the blinds. He inhaled deeply, the smoke swirling around him like a ghostly apparition, offering a temporary escape from the suffocating reality. His gaze, however, remained fixed on the bedroom door, where his mother and sister slept, their peaceful breaths a stark contrast to the storm raging inside him.

The room felt empty, a hollow shell of its former vibrancy. Only the three of them remained. The absence of Kam and Marcus hung heavy in the air, a constant, aching reminder of the shattered lives and broken dreams.

He knew he had to play his cards carefully. Trust was a luxury he could no longer afford. Every move, every word, every interaction was now a calculated maneuver in a game where the stakes couldn't be higher. He had to protect his family, dismantle the threat looming over them, and somehow, navigate the treacherous waters of his newfound reality.

Almost dozing off, the blunt slipped from his fingers, landing with a soft thud on the glass coffee table. He picked it up and extinguished it with a flick of his wrist. The silence amplified by the weight of his thoughts. He glanced at his phone, a tremor running through his hands. It vibrated, jolting him from his reverie. He fumbled around trying to answer and surprise crossed his face, then some relief. It was his uncle, Big D. He answered, his voice low.

 "You good, Unc, what's the move?"

A heavy silence hung in the air before Big D's voice rasped through the receiver, "I'm straight considering everything. We need to talk. I need to see you."

Jax's brow furrowed. "Where?" The usual spot was a relic of a past they couldn't afford to revisit.

Big D replied, his voice gruff, "I'll send you the location. Be there in an hour." He hung up before Jax could respond, leaving him staring at the phone, a knot of unease tightening in his stomach. What did Big D want? What information did he possess? And what did this unexpected meeting signify? Jax knew this wasn't a casual get-together. The urgency in Big D's voice, the abruptness of the call, it all pointed to something significant. Something dangerous. Honestly, he didn't want to dare leave Mecia and Ke' alone but the circumstances called for it.

He rose from the sofa, his movements fluid and deliberate, each muscle tense. He moved towards the door, his hand hovering over the doorknob. He needed to gather his thoughts, to prepare for the meeting with his uncle. The storm was brewing, and he, like the phoenix, had to be ready to rise from the ashes, stronger, more ruthless, more determined than ever before.

He exited the house, fought his way past the throng of news reporters and paparazzi that had gathered outside, and sped away from the scene, the engine of his car roaring like a caged beast ready for the moment of release.

Chapter 7
Unfinished Business

The afternoon heat laid beat down on the cracked asphalt of the narrow dirt road, casting long, skeletal shadows as Jax navigated his Chiron deeper into the desolate landscape. He regretted every mile his luxurious car had to endure in this terrain, but he had bigger problems. The atmosphere was heavy with dust and the only sound was the rhythmic thump of his tires against the unforgiving rocks in the road.

Following the cryptic instructions provided by Big D, he'd driven for what felt like an eternity, the vibrant city of Lubbock fading into a distant memory, swallowed by the encroaching darkness. Now, he found himself at the edge of Buffalo Lake, the shimmering expanse of water a stark contrast to the barren, windswept landscape that surrounded it. A single, skeletal tree stood sentinel, its branches clawing at the sky, a mournful testament to the unrelenting winds.

Jax parked the Chiron under the meager shade of the lone cottonwood tree, a knot of unease tightening in his stomach. The air here was thick with an oppressive stillness, broken only by the occasional croak of a lone frog and the unsettling whisper of the wind through the dry grass. He felt a shiver crawl down his spine.

His senses on high alert. Each rustle of leaves, each snap of a twig, sent a jolt of adrenaline coursing through him. He cautiously followed the overgrown path, the undergrowth scratching at his clothes, the silence broken only by the crunch of twigs beneath his shoes. Finally, through the dense foliage, he spotted it – an abandoned fishing shack, its paint peeling and its windows boarded up.

This was it. This was where Big D wanted him. Jax approached the shack, his hand reaching for the rusty latch on the raggedy door. He took a deep breath, his mind racing. What awaited him inside? What information did Big D possess? And what were the potential consequences of this meeting? The fate of his family, perhaps even the fate of the city, might hang in the balance.

With a grunt of effort, he pushed open the creaking door and stepped into the dim, musty interior. Dust caked the entirety of the shack's insides and a small break of light pierced through a cracked window, illuminating the cavernous space in an eerie, ethereal glow. Cobwebs clung to the walls like ghostly appendages, and the scent of fish decay lingered about.

He stood there for a moment, his eyes adjusting to the darkness, listening intently for any sound, any sign of life. The silence was deafening, punctuated only by the extreme pounding of his own heart.

Suddenly, a voice raspy with disuse echoed through the gloom. "About time you got here," as they stepped out of the shadows.

Jax whirled around, his hand instinctively reaching for the pistol holstered at his hip. But instead of the shadowy figure he expected, he was met with an unexpected sight. Standing before him, silhouetted against the dim light filtering through the grimy window, were three figures: Big D, flanked by Tina and Angela.

Jax stared at them, his mind reeling.

Big D stepped forward, his face etched with a pure determination. "Let's get down to business, nephew. Things have taken a turn for the worse."

Jax remained silent, his gaze fixed on his uncle, a wave of unease washing over him.

Big D continued, "You been seeing that shit about the bombing at the precinct, right?" Asking like they weren't both there. Jax nodded, his voice low "All night long."

"Yeah, well, some of them died. But not all of them." Big D paused, a chilling silence hanging in the air. "Sullivan's alive."

The blood drained from Jax's face. Sullivan. The dirty cop, the one who had who had killed Marcus and ruined his uncle's life was still breathing.

"We missed him," Big D confirmed, his voice a low growl. "He was placed administrative leave and left the building just before the bombing. That muthafucka got lucky! I don't know what would make him retaliate against me after all this time but it's the only thing that makes sense to me. All this shit is happening because of what I did. The man is killing everyone because of me nephew," Big D paused then continued. "It's a stretch but I think he may have even gotten Les' taken out too," Big D speculated. "I'm not one hundred percent positive on any of this but I'm trying to make it all make sense and to me it all fits."

A cold rage surged through Jax. Sullivan was still a threat. A threat they needed to eliminate. "Wait a minute, Unc," Jax cut in. "Les is dead too?"

"Shit was ruled an accident, but Tina saw a few things going on that could prove otherwise," Big D informed.

"Damn," Jax shook his head. The pressure mounting. "What do you want me to do, Unc?" Jax asked, his voice dangerous.

Big D smiled, a chilling, predatory smile. "I want you to help me finish what we started."

This was it. This was the chance to avenge his brother, to right the wrongs of the past. He nodded, a single thought dominating his mind: Sullivan was going to pay.

"Good," Big D said, his eyes gleaming in the dim light. "He's been a thorn in our side for too long. It's time to remove the thorn."

Tina, her face pale, stepped forward, her eyes filled with a mixture of fear and determination. "Are you sure about this, Jax?" She asked, her voice trembling slightly. "This is dangerous." Her connection to Jax deeper than what was on the surface.

Jax turned to look at her, his gaze unwavering. "This isn't just about revenge, Tina," he said, his voice low. "We owe that to Marcus, to Kam and anyone who has suffered because of this muthafucka."

Angela, her face a mask of concern, placed a hand on Jax's arm. "Be careful, Jax," she whispered. "We can't lose you too."

Jax squeezed her hand, a silent promise passing between them. "I'll be fine," he assured her, his voice firm. "I have to do this."

Big D nodded, a satisfied glint in his eyes. "Good. Now, let's discuss the plan." He gestured towards a crude map of the city sprawled out on a weathered wooden table. We need to find him and do the deed before it's too late. I have a feeling with all this crazy shit going on we have to hit now or he's gone be in the wind and walk free. I know this is gonna be really risky but what other options do we have?"

To be honest, everyone is that room had a weird vibe and was truly uncomfortable in their position, but no one protested against D's plan even though the timing and details of the plan seemed off. And so, the meeting continued, with the promise of danger and the hope of retribution. Jax, fueled by a potent mix of rage and grief, listened intently as Big D laid out their plan, a chilling smile playing on his lips. The hunt was on.

Chapter 8

The Seed of Doubt

"Alright, here's the plan. Sullivan's farmhouse is out in the countryside of the city completely isolated. We hit him there."

Jax's chest tightened, a cold fist squeezing his ribs. The plan, laid out with nefarious simplicity, felt wrong, bone-deep. A tremor ran through him, a premonition of disaster clinging to him like a shroud. "Unc," he began, his voice rough, "I don't know about this."

Big D scoffed, his gaze hardening. "What's wrong with you, nigga? I know you're itching for this just as bad as I am."

"It's not that," Jax insisted, "It just… it feels wrong. This whole thing… it feels too impulsive. Like we trying too hard."

Big D waved a dismissive hand. "We can't let this opportunity slip away. Sullivan's a loose end, a threat to everything we've built and our loved ones blood is on his hands!"

"But what if… what if something goes wrong?" Jax persisted, his voice rising. "What if we get caught? What if one of us gets hurt? Then who gone be here for my momma and my sister?"

Big D's eyes narrowed. "There will be no accidents. We'll be in and out before anyone even knows what hit them. He lives alone, unguarded. Maybe we get lucky and catch him while he's sleeping. Either way, the last thing I'm worried about is one of us getting hurt, nephew, that's no issue. But I get how you feel about your mom and sister, that's understandable."

Jax felt a surge of frustration, the taste of dust and stale air filling his mouth. His uncle was blinded by his own thirst for vengeance, unwilling to see the potential dangers. "Unc, I don't think this is the right way. We need to think this through. Breaking into this man's home is just… it's dangerous right now. We really don't know what's going on."

Big D slammed his fist on the table, the old wood groaning in protest. "Now, you're starting to sound like your old man, always second-guessing me and shit. This is how we survive in this world, Jax. You eliminate the threats before they eliminate you."

The anger in his uncle's eyes chilled Jax to the bone. He knew arguing further would be futile. Big D was a man of action, a man who believed in swift and decisive justice, even if it meant walking a dangerous line. He had a lil slick comment comparing Jax to his father. But Jax didn't know that nigga from a can of paint so he disregarded the remark.

"Fine," Jax conceded, his voice a mere whisper. "But I'm not involved on this one." He stood firm on his decision.

Big D's expression softened slightly. " You get back to the girls, keep them safe. Make sure they good. I got this. This is my fight."

Jax felt a strange sense of relief, even as a wave of guilt washed over him. He was abandoning his uncle, leaving him to face the danger alone. But he couldn't bring himself to participate in something he felt deep down was going to go wrong and leave his mother and sister alone to fend for themselves. With a heavy heart, Jax watched as his uncle and the ladies disappeared into the brush. He remained in the shack, the silence now deafening, the weight of his decision pressing down on him like a physical burden. He had chosen the path of inaction, wondering if could truly live with the consequences, especially if something went wrong? A shiver ran down his spine. This was not the end of this story, he knew. This was just the beginning of another chapter; one filled with uncertainty and the lingering shadows of doubt.

Chapter 9
Up In Smoke

The thick haze of marijuana smoke clung to the walls, a suffocating shroud over the bright television screen. News reports flashed across it, crystal clear images of frantic police officers and distraught citizens. Terry, with an almost manic glee, cackled as he passed the blunt to his sister.

"Did you see their faces?" He howled, pointing at the screen. "They look like they've seen a ghost! Or maybe two!" He let out another peel of laughter, smoke curling from his lips like a dragon's breath.

Tory, her eyes gleaming with a twisted delight, took a long drag from the blunt. "They're clueless," she sneered, exhaling a cloud of smoke that swirled around her head like a demonic halo. "Those cops wouldn't find a clue if it bit them on their asses."

Bundle, watching them from the corner of the room, shifted uncomfortably. He couldn't shake the lingering scent of burnt flesh and the echo of the explosion. "Don't get cocky," he warned, his voice a low growl. "This ain't over."

Terry scoffed, waving a dismissive hand. "Relax, Bundle. We were too smart for them. No witnesses, no evidence. In the midst of everything going on, really it's the perfect crime."

"Yeah," Tory chimed in, her voice dripping with sarcasm. "They'll be searching for years and come up empty. We're practically ghosts." Her dark humor was quite evident.

Terry leaned back, a smug grin plastered on his face. "We're free, Bundle. Free to do whatever we want. No more hiding, no more fear." He let out a whoop of joy, throwing his arms wide. "The world is ours!"

Bundle, however, couldn't quite share their enthusiasm. The weight of their actions pressed down on him, a heavy burden he couldn't shake off.

"Freedom?" he muttered, a bitter taste in his mouth. "This ain't freedom. This is just the beginning of a whole new nightmare. Do y'all not realize Lubbock is so fucked up right now they might call in the coast guard, pull in military help and may even declare for Martial Law?"

Tory rolled her eyes. "Oh, lighten up, Bundle. We did what we had to do. It's time to celebrate!" She grabbed the remote and cranked up the volume on the TV, the news anchor's panicked voice filling the room.

Terry jumped up, grabbing a half-empty bottle of whiskey from the floor. "Yeah, let's celebrate!" He shouted, taking a swig from the bottle. "To freedom! To revenge! To the chaos we've created!" He thrust the bottle towards Bundle, who hesitated for a moment before taking a reluctant gulp. The burning liquid did little to ease the unease churning in his stomach.

As Terry and Tory continued their twisted celebration, Bundle couldn't help but feel a growing sense of dread. He knew this was just the beginning. The consequences of their actions would come back to haunt them, sooner or later.

"Hey, Bundle," Terry called out, interrupting his thoughts. "Don't forget about your reward." He gestured towards two bulky sealed bags lying on the coffee table.

Bundle's eyes widened when he peeked in and recognized the contents: stacks of cash and the automatic shotgun he favored. "Damn," he breathed, a flicker of greed momentarily overshadowing his fear.

"That's all you, my man," Terry said with a grin. "You earned it."

Tory smirked. "Don't spend it all in one place."

"Actually, I just might," Bundle countered, a rare smile touching his lips.

"You know my momma's gonna have to undergo some chemo and radiation treatments for her cancer. And this right here," he hefted the bag of cash, "Will do wonders for the initial payments."

A flicker of surprise crossed Terry's face, quickly replaced by a nod of understanding. "Right on, man. Family first."

Tory, for once, seemed to soften slightly. "Hope your momma gets better."

Bundle nodded, a wave of warmth washing over him despite the grim circumstances. "Thanks." He couldn't deny the thrill of the reward, the promise of a new life, a life free from the current financial ruin he was in, and the chance to help his mother.

But as he left the twins' chaotic den, a nagging doubt lingered in his mind. Were their actions justified and called for? Was this deed of revenge worth the inevitable backlash? Had this been the defining moment that would propel them from the depths of the hole they were in or did they dig a bit deeper.

With that thought, he got himself together and shook the spot.

Chapter 10
Silent Traps

The Mercedes-Benz, a sleek white beast against the fading daylight, glided along desolate backroads, lined with skeletal trees and overgrown weeds, the moon casting long, eerie shadows. Inside, the air crackled with a mix of anticipation and shared resolve.

Big D, his face a mask of grim determination, gripped the steering wheel tight, his massive hands consuming the entire wheel. Beside him, Tina's eyes gleamed with a cold, predatory light. She checked her weapon, a silenced 9mm tucked neatly into the waistband of her jeans. Angela sat in the backseat, leaning forward, her hand intertwined with Tina's, her eyes burning with a fierce resolve, mirroring her lover's determination.

They were on their way to Sullivan's farmhouse, a secluded property deep in the heart of the countryside. Their plan was simple: a swift, silent strike. Big D would approach under the cover of the growing darkness and eliminate the detective and return to the car. Revenge, served cold and brutal, was their only motivation.

Sullivan, oblivious to the impending doom, had just poured himself a steaming cup of coffee. The aroma of freshly brewed coffee filled the small kitchen of his farmhouse with vibrant, calming energy, a stark contrast to the chilling paranoia that had gripped him since this whole ordeal with Marcus' death. The explosion at the precinct, the near miss on his life, the constant reports and questions from the public about the pending investigation – were beginning to take their toll. He was jumpier now, always on edge, a shadow of his former self.

Over the years following his wife's death, Detective Sullivan had fortified his property, a series of silent traps triggered by the slightest disturbance. Motion sensors, tripwires, and hidden cameras watched over his domain, a silent testament to his newfound paranoia. He'd become a spook, a shadow, always watching, always waiting. He glanced out the window, a look of unease crossing his face. He swore he heard the cracking of gravel in the road.

As the Benz crept closer to the farmhouse, the first trap was sprung. A hidden tripwire, buried deep in the overgrown grass, sent a silent signal to Sullivan's hidden surveillance system. The farmhouse, seemingly peaceful and idyllic, was a fortress of solitude, built because of the ever-present threat of violence that came with Sullivan's job and past history.

Meanwhile, Big D, a silent predator, moved with such uncanny grace through the underbrush. His massive frame seemed to melt into the shadows around him, his movements fluid and almost supernatural for a man of his size. He reached the edge of the property, his eyes scanning the windows of the farmhouse.

Inside, Sullivan, alerted by the tripwire, grabbed his shotgun from beneath the kitchen table. His heart hammered against his ribs, a frantic drumbeat against the silence of the farmhouse. He hadn't felt this surge of adrenaline since... well, since he killed Marcus Cook. He moved to the window, peering out into the darkness, his breath fogging the cold glass.

He saw a figure moving through the trees, a hulking silhouette against the pale moonlight. No, it couldn't be. It couldn't possibly be. But as the figure drew closer, a chilling recognition washed over him. That massive frame, the way it moved with such precision. It was none other than Big D.

"He's alive? But how?" Sullivan thought. They said he was dead. Died right in the prison cell where he'd sent him all those years ago. A wave of dizziness hit Sullivan, and he gripped the windowsill for support with one hand still holding his weapon in the other. This was impossible. It was a true was a nightmare.

He's come for me. The realization hit him like a punch to the gut. Big D was here for revenge. For his life! Panic clawed at his throat, choking him. He couldn't fight him. Not here. Not now. He was outmatched in comparison to his rival. His gaze darted around the room, searching for an escape route, a way out of this nightmare.

The barn. The truck. A desperate plan formed in his mind. He wouldn't fight. He would run. He would disappear into the night, leaving Big D to chase ghosts. He fumbled for his keys, his hands shaking so violently he could barely grip them. He fled the house, slipping out the back door and sprinting towards the barn, his boots pounding against the dirt. He jumped into his truck, the engine roaring to life like a startled beast. He threw it in gear and slammed his foot on the accelerator, tires spitting gravel as he sped away plummeting straight through the barn entrance, leaving the farmhouse behind, the devil inside.

***

Back at the Mercedes-Benz, Tina and Angela waited, their eyes fixed on the road ahead, their ears straining for any sound, any indication of what was happening. The only sound was the rhythmic thump of the Mercedes-Benz engine and the soft, rhythmic beat of their own pounding hearts.

Tina reached over and took Angela's hand, offering a silent reassurance. "He'll be alright," she whispered, but the tremor in her voice betrayed her own fear.

Out of nowhere, they heard a small crash and the sounds of a vehicle speeding away. They knew something was wrong and started to look around in panic. Shortly after, Big D arrived back to the car, breathing heavily.

"Go!" he yelled as he opened the door. "C'mon hurry we gotta get the fuck up outta here."

"What happened, are you okay?" Both women asked almost simultaneously.

"Fuck!" Big D slammed his heavy fist onto the dashboard as the car started flying down the dirt road.

"Talk to us babe what happened, D?" Angela questioned from the back, on the edge of her seat.

"We were too late. I barely missed that muthafucka! But he had a security system. The camera looked dead at me. I ain't cover my face like I was coming to rob him. I was coming for that muthafuckas life. Didn't expect him to slip away. Now I missed my chance to get him and if that footage gets out and the laws know I'm alive—"

Sharp headlights pierced the darkness behind them, approaching with alarming speed. A police car, its siren wailing, materialized seemingly out of thin air, screeching to a halt behind the Mercedes.

Big D's eyes widened in disbelief. They hadn't counted on this. Unbeknownst to them, just as Big D was ironically stating Sullivan's security system had captured Big D's image in crystal-clear 4K view as he forcefully entered the home. The footage was instantly broadcast to the authorities in real time, confirming with facial recognition software that Derrick Cook was not only alive but had just broken into the detective's home in an attempt to murder a police detective.

Before they had time to figure out what to do or discuss anything the pressure was on. The cop car now almost bumper to bumper meant business. The time was now either she needed to step on it and take their chances or pull over. For whatever reason she thought it would be best to choose the latter.

Tina, her face pale, gripped the steering wheel tightly, slowed down and pulled to the shoulder of the dirt road. It was dead silence in the car and no one moved a muscle as the officer behind exited the car." License and registration, please," she said, her voice remarkably steady despite the tremor running through her.

"Um, may I ask why you're pulling us over, officer?" Tina kept a straight face as she questioned stalling trying to somehow gauge this chance encounter.

The officer, a young white woman with short, cropped hair and sharp eyes, approached the car cautiously. She shone her flashlight into the vehicle, the beam briefly illuminating Big D's imposing figure. Her hand instinctively moved towards her holster as her voice wavered slightly.

"We received a disturbance call in the area, ma'am. Possible trespassers. Just a routine check." She paused, her gaze lingering on Big D, her eyes widening with certain recognition. She tried to take a few steps back and discreetly through some words over her shoulder into the walkie

"Dispatch, we might have a situation here. Possible sighting of... Derrick Cook. Requesting immediate backup," er voice low and tight with tension.

Angela, in the back seat, felt a chill crawl down her spine. She caught the officer's words and the urgency in her voice. This was not just a routine stop. This officer knew exactly who they were.

The officer continued her charade, shining her flashlight across the backseat, lingering on Angela's face. "You two seem a little tense," she observed, her voice strained. "Anything you'd like to tell me?"

Tina felt a bead of sweat trickle down her temple. This was not going as planned. The officer's stall tactics were becoming increasingly obvious. She was clearly waiting for backup, and Angela knew they couldn't risk being caught.

"Well, officer," Tina began, her voice calm despite the pounding of her heart against her ribs, "We were just out for a late-night drive. Enjoying the cool air. Is there anything in particular that seems amiss?"

The officer, her eyes narrowing, stepped closer to the car. "Just a feeling, ma'am. A gut feeling. Something's not quite right." She glanced at Big D, who remained eerily silent, his eyes fixed on a point in the distance.

"Perhaps you could step out of the vehicle for a moment? Just a routine check, as I said, while I wait on backup to arrive."

Angela's mind raced. This was a trap. They were being set up. The thought of losing D after everything they had been through, after all the sacrifices to free him and all the chaos engulfing their family, was unbearable. She couldn't let that happen.

With a sudden, unexpected move, Angela reached into her purse and pulled out her own weapon, a small but deadly .38 caliber. The officer, caught completely off guard, reacted instinctively, but it was too late. A single shot rang out, the sound echoing through the night. The officer slumped to the ground, a motionless figure in the dust.

Tina and Big D stared in awe at Angela. They hadn't expected this. The night, once filled with the promise of satisfying revenge, had erupted into further chaos. What more could go wrong?

Chapter 11
Mysterious Ways

The metallic clang of the commissary cart echoed down the pod, the noisy intrusion waking up grown men out of a deep sleep all around the jail. Tuck, perched on the edge of his bunk eating a bag of Whole Shabang Chips, watched the ensuing pandemonium with a weary sigh. Inmates surged forward, a sea of desperate faces all fighting for a good position, elbows flying as they scrambled to be first in line. Air crackled with a nervous energy, a volatile mix of anticipation and aggression, the usual.

"Man, if these niggas put this same kind of energy into their criminal defense or into anything other..." Tuck muttered to himself, the rest of the thought trailing off. He wasn't one for the drama, the constant posturing and the bravado that permeated this concrete jungle. He'd seen it all before – the braggadocio, the fleeting alliances, the fragile peace that could shatter at any moment in there.

He glanced at the line, the inmates vying for the instant gratification of overpriced ramen, sugary drinks, and those pathetically small bags of chips. It all seemed so pointless now. He used to be King Ding-a-Ling at the commissary, splurging on snacks, trying to maintain a semblance of normalcy. But lately, that whole charade felt hollow. Every day and dollar spent reminded him of how far he was away from his freedom and from getting back to his life. And honestly in his situation that day may never come. A flash of melancholy hit him. He thought of Jax, one of his best friends, struggling to cope with life's recent tragedies. Marcus, his little brother gone, another young life lost. Kam, his little sister, a superstar, silenced by a random and cowardly act of violence. His radio had blared all night, the newscaster's voice a grim monotone as she detailed the bombing, the city in a state of shock.

Tuck remembered the days not long ago when they were all young, running the streets, dreaming big. Always pushing to strive for more, to escape the confines of this city. Now, Greedy and D-Lee were gone, victims of the same streets they had once navigated with such bravado.

The struggles in the commissary line continued unabated, the problem micro in comparison to the larger chaos that seemed to have enveloped the city. Tuck closed his eyes, the memories flooding back –from all those nights in the trap making plays, to the late nights at the studio with Kam and '3BG', their voices blending in perfect harmony. The thrill of their first live performance, the intoxicating scent of success. Now, that music, that vibrant energy was gone, extinguished by more violence.

He felt a surge of anger, a desperate yearning to break free from this suffocating environment, to do something, anything, to help Jax, and to honor the memory of his fallen friends. But what could he do from here? Trapped in this concrete box, his options were limited. Yet, defiance ignited within him. He wouldn't let this time defeat him. He would find a way out, a way to make a difference, even from behind these bars.

Finally, Tuck pushed himself off the bunk, the worn mattress groaning in protest. The metallic clang of the cart seemed to echo forever, a constant reminder of the mundane reality of his existence. He couldn't stay cooped up in the cell forever.

The energy emanating from the line was a strange mix of desperation and the camaraderie was oddly compelling.

Besides, cold soda sounded pretty good. He slipped into the line, maneuvering smooth through the throng of inmates, thick with the scent of sweat and regret. He found a spot near the back, a quiet refuge away from the boisterous arguments and the simmering tension.

Suddenly, a gruff voice broke from the man in front of him.

"What's wrong with your face, nigga? We know your books loaded?"

Tuck looked up to see an older inmate, his face a roadmap of wrinkles, his eyes twinkling with mischief.

"Old Man Nick," he acknowledged, a level of respect coloring his tone.

"You'll be home soon," Old Man Nick declared, his voice surprisingly firm. "Real soon."

Tuck scoffed. "Home soon? Man, school you trippin'. Dem Folks might fuck around and give me the needle." He gestured vaguely towards the front of the line, where a heated argument was brewing. They watched until it fizzled out then carried on.

Old Man Nick chuckled, a low rumble in his chest. "See, that's the problem with you youngsters. You worry too much. Don't know how to keep faith. You pay attention to what you want to pay attention to, instead of what you should be paying attention to." He didn't say much else as the line progressed, patiently waiting for his turn.

When the old man finally made it to the commissary window, he slid the lady his ID card and short item list on a hope he could get what he wanted. Sometimes his money was there, sometimes it wasn't. That was just the case sometimes with incarceration, you could look out for the entire family on the outs and really be one to hold it down, but if there came the time you were down, you might be shit outta luck.

"Sorry Pop, no funds. Try again next week," The Commissary lady said to him with a look of pity.

Old Man Nick knew the drill, no stranger to the walk of shame. Unfazed, he held his head high and went on about his business to his normal reserved spot in the dayroom by the TV.

Tuck stepped up to the window next slid his ID to the lady, she scanned it and was immediately taken aback by the outrageous balance. She gazed up with mouthwatering interest and Tuck responded with a knowing wink. "Aye, what was Old Man tryna get?"

"Uh, just two black bags of coffee. Why are you gonna get it for him? Looks like you definitely can." The Commissary lady giggled.

"Yeah, hook my man up and just add it to my list would you?" Tuck shot back as he gave her his list through the slot. They exchanged knowing glances throughout the rest of the transaction and the lady secretly added something extra for him to find later if he checked his receipt.

He got his bag, hefted it over his shoulder and before he even took it back in the cell he pulled up on Old Man Nick sitting at the table and dropped the two bags of coffee on em'.

The Old Man looked up with surprise and abundance of gratitude smiling from ear to ear his dentures on full display. "Good looking, youngster!"

"No thang, school." Tuck raised an eyebrow, "Earlier what you mean, 'should be paying attention to'?"

Old Man Nick leaned closer, his eyes gleaming with a knowing light. "They've been talking about it on the news all day, son. Haven't you been paying attention?" He lowered his voice, "That explosion at the police station... it's gonna change everything."

Tuck frowned, confused. "What you talkin' 'bout, Old Man? How's that gonna change anything for us in here?"

Old Man Nick's smile widened. "Think about it, boy. They lost half their force in that blast. And ain't nobody talking about the evidence room..." He paused, letting the implication hang in the air.

Tuck's eyes widened. "The evidence room? You think...?"

"I know," Old Man Nick interrupted, his voice a hoarse whisper. "All that evidence... gone. Up in smoke. Cases are gonna start getting thrown out left and right. Yours included."

Tuck felt a surge of hope, a flicker of light in the darkness that had surrounded him. He thought about Jax, about his family and other associates, about the possibility of returning to the world outside these walls.

Old Man Nick continued, his voice gaining strength. "They ain't got nothin' on you no more, Tuck. No evidence, no witnesses to says you're the exact one did whatever it is they says ya' done. So look out now... you're a free man!"

Tuck stared at him, a mix of disbelief and elation swirling within him. Could it be true? Could he really walk out of here? He thought about all the years lingering ahead to be spent behind bars, the time to be stolen from him, the opportunities to be missed.

Old Man Nick clapped him on the shoulder, a wide grin on his face. "Mark my words, boy. You'll be home soon. Real soon."

Tuck nodded, a newfound determination burning in his eyes. He would call his lawyer, fight for his freedom, and return to the world that had been taken from him. He would honor the memory of his fallen friends and be there for those who needed him and make things right.

Chapter 12
The Last Laugh

Bundle slid behind the wheel of his red Chevy Caprice, the weight of the cash heavy in his lap. The car sputtered to life, its engine coughing and wheezing like an old man with a bad cold. But that wouldn't be an issue much longer due to his new windfall.

He glanced at the rearview mirror, the image of the twins' house fading into the distance. Their world, their problems, their chaos - it was all starting to feel distant the further he drove, almost unreal.

A surge of satisfaction found him. The money, the thrill of the kill, the power it gave him - it was intoxicating. But beneath the euphoria, a darker, more sinister satisfaction lurked. He thought about Jax, about his smug smile, his arrogance. Bundle had always resented him, envied his success, his connections, his family. But now that he had a taste of revenge, he was happy. Although that taste left him wanting a little more.

His mind drifted to Kenny, his older brother, the man who had always looked out for him. Kenny, with his charm and cunning, had been the perfect partner for this scheme. They'd been planning this for months, a twisted plot against Jax, to kidnap his son, Jr. and hold him for ransom. Kenny was supposed to use his charm to get close to Cori, Jax's baby mama, gain her trust, and they would rely upon that connection to get close enough to snatch the kid.

But then, Kenny had gone and fallen for Cori. Actually fallen for her. Bundle had been furious. Cori, with her expensive tastes and ever-shifting moods, was a liability. She was high-maintenance, paranoid, and constantly questioning Kenny's every move. It was like Kenny had forgotten the whole damn plan, blinded by some misguided infatuation. With that, it's like once Cori realized how Kenny was, she pushed away and the whole relationship quickly imploded.

"Emotions ruin the job," Bundle muttered to himself, shaking his head. He'd always prided himself on his pragmatism, his ability to separate business from personal feelings. But Kenny... Kenny had let his emotions get the better of him.

He'd let Cori distract him from the prize. Then she broke it off with him and the whole Kidnapping for ransom plan was shot. Then, just when it seemed like their plan was falling apart, fate had intervened. The twins, with their own vendetta against Jax, had offered Bundle a chance to get his revenge and get paid in the process. With Kenny and Cori officially over, there was nothing holding him back anymore.

He couldn't deny that a part of him was disappointed that their original plan had failed. Kidnapping Jax's son would have been the ultimate payback, a blow that would have shattered Jax's world and would have easily brought them millions if they executed the plan precisely. But fifty thousand dollars was nothing to sneeze at. Plus the emotional pain he'd inflicted on Jax, the fear and uncertainty he'd sown in his heart, was far more valuable than any amount of money.

As he drove, his mind raced with new possibilities. He thought about his momma, battling cancer with little hope and even less money. This cash could change everything. It could pay for her treatments, give her a fighting chance. A warmth spread through him, a feeling he hadn't experienced in a long time.

He pictured himself opening a small business, maybe a garage or a body shop. He'd always been good with his hands, and this money could be the seed for a legitimate future, a way out of the cycle of violence and poverty that had plagued his family and so many others for generations.

He pulled up to Kenny's house, a modest apartment on the East side of town, right of MLK Dr. across the street from Estacado High School. As he stepped out of the car, a nostalgic feeling graced him. It had been years since he'd been able to really put true thought into something positive for their future.

He knocked on the door, and a moment later, Kenny appeared, his face lit up with surprise. "Bundle! Man, what's up lil big bro? You look like you just won the lottery."

Bundle grinned. "You could say that." He handed Kenny the bag of cash, a silent acknowledgment of their shared success, even if it wasn't the success they'd originally planned for.

Kenny's eyes widened as he weighed the bag in his hands. "This gotta be at least like what forty-fifty grand? Damn, nigga, where'd you pull this off?"

Bundle shrugged. "A little hustle here and there." He didn't want to share the details of his involvement with the twins, not yet.

"Well, whatever you did, I'm not complaining," Kenny said with a grin.

"This could change everything."

As they sat down to discuss their next move, Bundle couldn't help but feel a sense of satisfaction. He had played his cards right, and now, the future was wide open. He would use this money, this opportunity, to build a new life for himself, a life free from the shadows and the pain of the past. Most importantly when it came to him and Jax, Bundle reveled in the thought of having the last laugh. He was cool with that.

Chapter 13
Can't Catch a Break

Jax's Chiron tires screeched to a halt in front of Mecia's house, the engine's battle cry swallowed by the swirl of sirens and flashing lights that assaulted his senses. He'd left the meeting with Big D feeling a knot of unease in his stomach, a premonition of something bad looming. Now, as he slammed the car door shut, the scene before him confirmed his worst fears.

The street was a chaotic tableau of flashing blue and red, a swarm of police cruisers and ambulances casting an eerie glow on the familiar houses on the block. Reporters buzzing around like vultures drawn to carrion, battling for position, their cameras flashing, microphones thrust forward, eager to capture the latest tragedy unfolding in this cursed city.

Jax pushed his way through the throng, his heart pounding with a sickening dread. He saw paramedics rushing out of the house, their faces grim, carrying a stretcher bearing a still figure. His blood ran cold. He recognized the floral print of the nightgown. It was Mecia.

"Ma!" he screamed, his voice raw with panic. He pushed past the paramedics, his eyes frantically searching for any sign of life. Mecia lay motionless, her face pale, her breathing shallow.

Ke' came bounding out the front door, her eyes red and swollen, rushed towards him, clutching his arm. "Jax, she just... collapsed not long after she took her medicine. I called 911, but..." Her voice trailed off, choked with sobs.

Jax felt the nausea building. First his friends, then Marcus and Kam, now this. It was as if fate was determined to strip him of everything he held dear. He couldn't lose his mother, not now, not after everything they'd been through. He followed the paramedics as they loaded Mecia into the back of the ambulance, Ke' electing to ride inside with her. His mind was an unstable whirlwind of fear and desperation. He jumped into his car, ignoring pleas from the crowd to answer a few questions, and sped off after the ambulance, weaving through traffic with reckless abandon. He had to get to the hospital, had to be there for his mother, had to make sure she was okay.

***

The waiting room at the ER was a sterile, fluorescent-lit purgatory. Jax paced restlessly, his anxiety growing with each passing minute. Ke' sat beside him, her hand clutching his, her silence a heavy weight in the air. All they could do was wait patiently and pray that everything was okay. Even though there wasn't anything Jax could really do, he was already kicking himself in the ass for leaving them alone. The idea constantly chewed at him as time passed slowly.

***

Finally, a doctor emerged, his face etched with concern. "Family of Ms. Cook," he began, "your mother is stable for now, but..." He hesitated, his eyes filled with a gravity that sent a shiver down Jax's spine.

"But what?" Jax demanded, his voice sharp with hostility and displaced aggression.

"We've run some tests," the doctor continued, "and we've found something... unexpected." He paused, choosing his words carefully. "Seems as if your mother has accidentally been introduced to some foreign substance or has been intentionally poisoned. For now, she's stable, but with the dose of toxins in her system, and considering her existing health complications, we've had to admit her for observation to see how she is responding to treatment. We need to monitor her closely for now."

Jax stared at him, his mind reeling. Foreign substance? Poisoned? But how? Who? Again nothing that was happening made sense…

The doctor explained that the poison was a slow-acting toxin, one that had been accumulating in Mecia's system over time. It was likely the recent stress and trauma had exacerbated its effects, leading to her collapse.

Jax felt a surge of rage. Someone had deliberately poisoned his mother. But who? And why? Was this connected to the attacks on his family, or was this something else entirely?

Terrible things just kept happening so fast right after another he just didn't have the time to ever think things through. This was becoming the new normal and he wasn't adjusting well.

He looked at Ke', her eyes puffy and wet. He had to protect her, had to find out who was behind this, had to make them pay. This shit had to stop!

Jax pulled out his phone, his hands trembling as he dialed Big D's number. It went straight to voicemail. "C'mon man answer the muthafuckin' phone!" He hung up, tried again. Voicemail. A third attempt yielded the same result. Panic clawed at his throat. Where the hell was Big D? He needed answers, needed help, needed to know they weren't alone in this fight. But the unanswered calls only amplified his fear, a chilling reminder of how quickly things could spiral out of control.

Chapter 14
Nowhere to Run

The Mercedes-Benz, now a fugitive vessel, sped through the desolate night, its headlights cutting through the darkness like a pair knives. Inside, the atmosphere was thick with tension and fear. Big D slammed his fist against the dashboard on the passenger side, his face contorted in frustration. "Damn it, Angela! What the hell was you thinking?"

Tina, her hands still shaking from the encounter, trying her best to steer them clear, echoed his sentiment. "We had it under control. Now we've got a dead cop on our hands!"

Angela, scared but resolute, met their gaze. "And what was the fuckin' alternative, Huh! Let her arrest us? Let them take D back to that hellhole? After everything we've been through and us barely getting him back? What about Jax and the family? I did exactly what either of you would have done." Her voice cracked with raw emotion. "I wasn't going to lose him, not like this, fuck that!"

A knowing silence fell over the car. Big D, his anger subsiding, looked at Angela, his eyes filled with a mix of gratitude and fear. He knew she had acted impulsively, but he also understood her desperation and honestly appreciated the gesture. Hell, everything she'd done. Every sacrifice both women made just to get him to that point. This wasn't something to overlook. They were in a corner, and she had made a choice, a choice that had irrevocably changed their lives furthermore, but they couldn't fault her for that.

Tina, her worry taking over, turned on the radio. The news crackled to life, the announcer's voice a grim harbinger of their fate. *"...breaking news... a Lubbock County Police officer shot and killed during a routine traffic stop... suspects identified as Derrick Cook, escaped convict, said to be traveling with the likes of at least one other person, a woman who's been identified as Tina..."* The rest of the report was a blur of details, descriptions of their vehicle, warnings to the public.

Big D's face hardened. "They're broadcasting it everywhere," he growled. "Fuck!"

Angela's heart sank. She hadn't considered the consequences of her actions, the ripple effect that one impulsive decision could have. Now, they were fugitives, their faces plastered across every screen in the country. Ever the resourceful one, Angela pulled up the web on a screen in her in dash, scrolling through news sites and social media. "It's worse than we thought," she said, her voice grim. "They've already released the footage from Sullivan's house. Everyone knows you're alive, D. They're calling you a cop killer. They even have the dashcam video out. Man, this is crazy babe all this shit happening so fast!"

Big D slumped back in his seat, the weight of their situation crushing him.

He had escaped prison, only to find himself trapped in a different kind of hell.

"Where do we go?" Tina whispered, her voice filled with fear as she navigated the car. The question hung in the air, unanswered. They were adrift, lost in a sea of uncertainty, with nowhere to turn and nowhere to hide.

Suddenly, scaring the shit out of everyone... Big D's phone rang. He saw it was Jax calling but let the call go unanswered despite disputes from both women to pick it up. He just couldn't bring himself to tell his nephew what just happened and put more food on his plate. Sure enough, he would see for himself how real shit had gotten for the home team. But he didn't plan to leave him in the dark long. Just until he had some time to think clearly and figure out where to go moving forward.

"We can't go back to Lubbock," he said, his voice tight. "Not now. They'll be waiting for us."

Tina nodded, her face grim. "We need to disappear. Lay low until this blows over."

But where could they go? They were in West Texas, a vast expanse of desertish flatland, with few places to hide. Every town, every gas station, every motel was a potential trap.

"We need a plan," Angela said, her voice shaking but determined. "We need to think this through."

They drove in silence for a while, the only sound the hum of the engine and the occasional crackle of the radio. The news reports were relentless, each update painting a grimmer picture of their situation. They were public enemies now, their faces plastered across every screen in the county.

"We need to get off this highway and exit here," Tina said, breaking the silence. "Stick to the back roads, avoid any towns."

Big D nodded. "We need to find somewhere safe, somewhere they won't think to look for us."

But where? The question gnawed at them, a constant reminder of their precarious situation. They were running out of time, running out of options.

As the night wore on, the landscape grew increasingly desolate. The highway gave way to narrow dirt roads, winding through endless fields of cotton and corn.

The occasional farmhouse flickered in the distance, isolated beacons in the vast darkness.

"We can't keep driving aimlessly," Angela said, her voice laced with anxiety.

"We need a destination."

Big D sighed, his frustration mounting. "I know, I know. But I can't call in my sources on this one. Even though they could bail us out of this in a heartbeat, I don't right now I'll qualify for those services." This statement alone hinting at a possible issue and threat bigger than the current.

Angela thought for a moment, her eyes scanning the passing landscape.

Suddenly, a thought struck her. "There's a place," she said, her voice gaining confidence. "A small town, just North of Lubbock. It's practically a ghost town now, but my family owns some land there. An old farmhouse, abandoned for years. No one would ever think to look for us there."

Tina and Big D exchanged glances. It was a long shot, but it was their only option.

"Which way?" Big D asked with a glimmer of hope dancing in his eyes.

Angela directed them off the main road, onto a narrow, barely visible track that snaked through the fields. The Mercedes bounced and swayed, its headlights struggling to penetrate far into the growing darkness.

After what seemed like an eternity, they reached a clearing. In the center stood a tall grey house, its paint peeling, some windows broken. It looked like something out of a horror movie, but to them, it was now sanctuary. They pulled up to the house, their headlights illuminating the overgrown yard and the crumbling porch. A sense of relief touching their souls. They had found a temporary haven, a place to catch their breath and plan their next move.

As they stepped out of the car, the silence of the night enveloped them. The only sound was the chirping of crickets and the distant howl of a coyote. For the first time in hours, they felt a sense of safety, a fragile respite from the chaos that had consumed their lives recently.

They knew this was just a temporary reprieve. They couldn't hide forever. But for now, they had a place to regroup, to gather their strength, and to face the challenges that lay ahead.

Chapter 15

The City of Angels and Demons

The studio lights beat down on Gabrielle Renee, they were hot and intense, like the scrutiny of a thousand eyes. She took a deep breath, adjusting the microphone on her lapel, the familiar weight, a comfort in this unfamiliar territory.

Tonight, she wasn't just reporting the news; she was narrating a tragedy, a saga of heartbreak and injustice that had gripped not only her city but the entire nation. And this was especially difficult for her because she knew this family. Sure, with Jax's status and who he had become, she doubted he remembered her. But he was a man she'd never forget. The way he carried himself, even back then in high school, with a quiet strength and determination that belied his youth. The way his eyes lit up when he talked about his dreams for the future, dreams that now seemed so distant, so cruelly snatched away.

Gabrielle's heart pounded against her ribs, a frantic drumbeat echoing the chaos that had consumed Lubbock. The teleprompter scrolled, a litany of names and dates, each one a fresh wound on the soul of their community and all circling back to one family. Marcus Cook, Kam Cook, Mecia Cook, Big D... the list seemed endless, a testament to the violence that had stained their streets and shattered countless lives.

She glanced at the monitor, the image of her own face staring back, serious and determined. Tonight, she was more than just a reporter; she was a voice for the voiceless, a conduit for the pain and frustration that simmered beneath the surface of their city. She was Gabrielle Renee', and she was about to tell the story of Jax and the Cook family, a story of angels and demons, of dreams and despair, a family caught in a perpetual crisis in a city teetering on the brink of collapse.

"Good evening, and welcome back," Gabrielle began, her voice steady despite the tremor in her hands. "Tonight, we delve deeper into the heart of darkness that has enveloped our city, a darkness that has claimed the lives of too many, leaving a trail of grief and unanswered questions."

The camera zoomed in, framing her face in a close-up. She could feel the weight of the nation's gaze, the collective breath held in anticipation. She continued, her voice gaining strength, "The Cook family, once a beacon of hope and resilience now stands as a symbol of our city's broken promises. Marcus Cook, a talented young athlete, gunned down in a hail of police bullets. Kam Cook, a rising music superstar, silenced by a cowardly act of terror by unknown perpetrators. And now, Mecia Cook, the matriarch of the family, fighting for her life after a suspected poisoning. The son, Jax White and youngest daughter Ke' Cook alive, but clearly suffering."

The images flashed across the screen – Marcus's smiling face frozen in time after scoring a touchdown. Kam's vibrant stage presence extinguished, Mecia's frail figure lying in a hospital bed. Each image a fresh stab of pain.

"These are not isolated incidents," Gabrielle emphasized, her voice rising with controlled anger. "They are part of a larger pattern of violence and corruption that has plagued our city for far too long but this family specifically. Just weeks ago DeMarco Lee, Byron Parker, close friends of the son, murdered in cold blood at a nightclub. Authorities have tried to sway the public into believing that those were committed by Marcus Cook, which played a part in his death at the hands of police. Another man associated with the family, Tuck Williams was jailed ... all these people with ties to this family unfortunately suffering in some way...and it seems the list of victims grows longer with each passing day, their blood crying out for justice."

She paused, letting the weight of her words sink in. The studio was silent. The only sound, the hum of the cameras and the frantic beating of her own heart.

Gabrielle continued, her voice gaining urgency, "The public is demanding answers. They want to know who is behind these attacks, what their motives are, and why the authorities seem powerless to stop them ... Everyone from government high ups to everyday citizens wants answers about the police precinct bombing. As crazy as it sounds, this story may be one in the same."

The screen switched to a montage of news clips – protests erupting in the streets, heated debates on talk shows, social media ablaze with outrage and speculation. Hashtags like #JusticeForCookFamily and #LubbockStrong trended nationwide, a testament to the widespread impact of the events and losses.

"There are theories upon theories spreading rampant," Gabrielle acknowledged, her voice measured. "Some whisper of political corruption, of powerful figures silencing those who threaten their interests. Others point to police retaliation, a desperate attempt to cover past misdeeds. And still others speak of personal vendettas between law enforcement and wanted man Derrick Cook in a cycle of violence that seems to have no end."

Gabrielle leaned forward, her gaze intense. "Amidst the chaos, a new twist has emerged, one that casts a long shadow over the Cook family. Derrick Cook, known as Big D, an ex-convict sentenced to life in prison and recently believed to be dead, has re-emerged. Though not as a grieving uncle seeking solace, but as a fugitive, a prime suspect in the attempted murder of a detective and the bombing of the Lubbock Police Department."

The screen displayed Big D's mugshot, his face etched with defiance and a hint of desperation. Gabrielle continued, her voice laced with a mix of fascination and dread, "Long ago the authorities linked Big D's possible ties to the infamous Corona Cartel, a shadowy organization with a reputation for ruthlessness and violence, upon pumping various drugs and making way for illicit activity in our country and community. It seems the Cook family is caught in a web of negative intrigue, their lives entangled with forces that may be beyond their control."

Gabrielle paused, the weight of the situation pressing down on her. "And as if the violence and accusations weren't enough, its being said in overnight reports leaked online that Jax's record label, once a symbol of success and innovation, is now facing a mass exodus of artists, some fearing their reputations will be tarnished by association and connection to the label. Which may or may not be the case seeing that current streaming numbers and sales have gone up for Hub City Records affiliates after the news on the tragic death of fellow artist, Kam, leader of the Grammy award winning group, "3BG". Despite that, the future of the label hangs precariously in the balance."

She shook her head, a show of realistic sympathy. "It seems the Cook family can't catch a break. Every step forward is met with a devastating setback, every glimmer of hope extinguished by the encroaching darkness."

Gabrielle's voice gained strength, fueled by a sense of injustice. "But amidst the despair, a spark of defiance remains. The Cook family, battered but not broken, refuses to surrender. They are fighting for their survival, for their legacy, for the justice they deserve."

She leaned forward, her eyes locked on the camera. "And we, the public, cannot stand idly by. We must demand answers, hold those in power accountable, and fight for a city where families like the Cooks can thrive, not merely survive."

Gabrielle took a deep breath, her heart still pounding. She had done her part, had shared the story, had given voice to the pain and outrage. Now, it was up to the authorities, to the public, to demand action, to bring the perpetrators to justice.

"This is Gabrielle Renee, reporting live from Lubbock, Texas," she concluded, her voice firm. "The city of angels and demons, where the battle for truth and justice rages on."

As the camera lights dimmed, exhaustion took over her. But beneath the fatigue, a burning ball of defiance remained. She wouldn't rest until the truth was revealed, until Jax, an old friend, found peace. Gabrielle knew the road ahead would be dangerous, but she was ready for the fight.

Chapter 16
The Shifting Sands

A calming rift of birdsong rang about, very tranquil in comparison to the tension that crackled within the opulent Mexican villa. The scent of hibiscus and saltwater hung heavy in the air, a fragrant reminder of the paradise Christo had carved out for himself on this secluded island. But even the gentle caress of the tropical breeze couldn't dispel the storm clouds gathering on the horizon.

Inside the villa, cool and serene despite the oppressive heat outside, Christo paced restlessly, the polished marble floor reflecting his agitated movements. News reports blared from the massive flat-screen television that dominated one wall, the images a jarring intrusion into the carefully curated tranquility of his sanctuary.

The chaos in Lubbock unfolded before his eyes—the bombed-out police precinct, the charred wreckage of Kam Cook's car Big D's mugshot on every station. Each scene a fresh wound on the city he once considered an extension of his own empire, each report a hammer blow to the carefully constructed image of control and invincibility he'd cultivated over decades.

Christo silenced the television with a sharp gesture, the sudden quiet amplifying the disquiet within him. He couldn't shake the feeling that this was more than just a series of unfortunate events. There was a pattern here, a deliberate hand guiding the chaos, and he was determined to uncover who was responsible.

This very person ruined the life he so rightfully deserved.

He moved to the expansive balcony overlooking the turquoise waters of the sea, the rhythmic crash of waves against the shore a soothing counterpoint to the turmoil brewing within him. He inhaled deeply, the salty air filling his lungs, a momentary respite from the suffocating weight of responsibility that pressed down on him.

Christo, a man whose roots ran deep into the rich soil of Mexico, a man who had navigated the treacherous currents of the Cartel world since his youth, felt a growing unease. He had always prided himself on his ability to anticipate and control events, to manipulate the players on the board to his advantage. But this situation in Lubbock was different, unpredictable, a wildfire burning out of control. He'd overestimated the ability of Jax and Big D to control their sector and doing so he found himself at a loss.

Now his very own position within the Cartel was precarious, his authority challenged by a council of Cartel bosses. Those who saw his ventures into Texas, his alliances with the "*Blacks*" as business associates, as a betrayal of their traditions, a dilution of their own power. They whispered behind his back, criticizing his methods, questioning his loyalty, undermining his every move.

The recent chaos in Lubbock had given the council the ammunition they needed. The financial losses, the unpaid debts, the tarnished reputation— it was all being used against him, a weapon wielded by his enemies to strip him of his power and influence.

He thought of Jax, the young protégé he'd once seen as a reflection of his younger self even more so than his uncle. Ambitious, ruthless, and hungry for power, Jax had been a valuable asset, a rising star in the Cartel's firmament for the last seven years. But now, Jax was a liability, his family a magnet for tragedy and unwanted attention.

Although technically this scenario could playout in anyone's life the recent events of Jax's tarnished his reputation with the Council. He was just seen to be jeopardizing their operations and eroding their influence. The new leadership, a faceless collective of investors and power brokers, was less tolerant of risk, more focused on the bottom line. The old ways of doing business, the favors and alliances built on trust and reputation, were being phased out, replaced by a cold, calculating pragmatism that left no room for sentimentality or error, period. And then there was Big D, the unpredictable wildcard. Christo had always loved Big D's loyalty. Their bond cemented since a chance encounter back in the early 90's that ultimately led to him taking Big D under his umbrella of success. When Big D stayed solid to the Cartel during his trial, he not only saved his own life but secured the connection to bestow the Cartel with a successor in his place when the time was right. However, his escape from prison and his alleged involvement in the police bombing without prior notice to the organization had thrown another wrench into the works, further complicating an already volatile situation.

Christo's frown deepened. He knew that Jax and Big D were expendable in the council's eyes. If they failed to resolve the situation in Lubbock, if they continued to attract unwanted attention and jeopardize the cartel's interests, they would be killed, no doubt about it. It was a harsh reality, but one that Christo had long since accepted too. True sentimentality had no place in his world, not when the stakes were this high.

He reached for his phone, his fingers tapping out Jax's number with a practiced ease. The line crackled to life, and Jax's voice, tense and apprehensive, filled the silence.

"Christo," Jax acknowledged, his voice barely a whisper.

"Si," Christo responded, his accent thick, "We need to talk, my friend."

He paused, letting the weight of his words sink in. Jax remained silent, his apprehension palpable. Christo continued, his voice gaining strength, "The situation in Lubbock has become untenable. The authorities are too close for comfort, and the media is relentless."

Jax's voice tightened. "I know, Christo. I'm trying to fix it."

"Trying isn't enough at this point, Jax," Christo interrupted, his tone hardening. "The new leadership is losing patience. They demand results, not excuses."

He paused again, letting the implication hang in the air. Jax's breath hitched.

Christo continued, his voice low and menacing, "The old ways of doing business are gone, Jax. The cartel is no longer a family. It's a machine, and machines don't tolerate inefficiency or disloyalty."

Jax's voice elevated, "So what you sayin', Christo?"

"I'm saying that you and your family are in danger, Jax," Christo replied, his voice devoid of emotion. "If you fail to resolve this situation, if you continue to jeopardize our interests, you will be eliminated."

"Eliminated?" Jax echoed, his voice rising in anger and disgust. "But I've been loyal, I've done everything you've ever asked—"

"Your loyalty is irrelevant, Jax," Christo cut him off, his voice cold and sharp. "The new leadership doesn't care about past favors or alliances. They care about results, about profit, about maintaining our position of power."

"But I can fix this," Jax pleaded, desperation creeping into his voice. "Just give me more time—"

"Time is a luxury we can no longer afford, Jax," Christo stated flatly. "The clock is ticking. You need to clean up this mess, and you need to do it quickly. Silence the critics, eliminate the threats, and restore our reputation. More importantly, you need to repay the debts you owe. The Cartel is not nor will it ever be a charity, Jax. We are a business, and we expect to be compensated for our services."

A wave of bitter anger took over Jax. "Debts!" He spat, his voice laced with disbelief. "You think this is about the fucking money? You think I can't pay what I owe? I've poured my life into this, into helping you expand your empire, and this is the thanks I get? Abandoned, left to fend for myself, while my family is being slaughtered?"

"Sentimentality has no place in this business, Jax. You know that better than anyone. The Cartel's interests come first. Always."

"And what about loyalty?" Jax challenged, his voice trembling with rage. "What about the years I've given you, the risks I've taken, the sacrifices I've made?"

"Loyalty is a two-way street, Jax," Christo countered, his voice laced with steel.

"And you've strayed from the path. You've become a liability, a threat to our operations. You need to prove your worth, Jax. You need to earn your redemption. Your fate is in your hands, Jax," Christo stated coldly. "Resolve this situation, and you will be spared. Fail, and all of will pay the price."

"And what about you?" Jax challenged, his voice dripping with contempt.

"My fate is my own concern, Jax," Christo retorted, his voice laced with arrogance. "Your concern is your family, and your survival. Don't confuse the two."

A cold dread gripped Jax's heart. Christo words were a death knell, a confirmation that he was truly alone in this fight. He had no allies, no protectors, only enemies closing in from all sides.

"So that's it then, huh" Jax asked "After all these years, after everything I've done, I'm just another pawn to be sacrificed?"

"Everyone is expendable, Jax," Christo stated flatly. "Even you. Especially now."

"And what about the shipment?" Jax blurted out, a sudden realization hitting him. "The one at the port? Do you even remember that?"

A flicker of surprise crossed Christo's face, quickly replaced by a mask of cold indifference. "The shipment is irrelevant, Jax. A minor setback, easily rectified. Your failures, however, are not so easily dismissed."

Jax's blood ran cold. He had forgotten about the shipment, a massive consignment of product due to be picked up that week. With everything that had happened, with the chaos and grief consuming him, it had slipped his mind. And now, it was another weapon in Cartel's arsenal, another reason to discard him.

"You're playing a dangerous game, Jax," Christo warned, his voice laced with steel. "Don't overestimate your importance. Don't underestimate my resolve."

He ended the call abruptly, the silence that followed heavy with unspoken threats. Christo tossed the phone onto the plush sofa, a grim satisfaction settling in his chest. He had delivered the message, and had made the threat clear. Now, it was up to Jax to earn his redemption. Or face the consequences.

Christo rose from his seat, his gaze sweeping across the opulent surroundings. The villa, with its lavish furnishings and breathtaking views, was a symbol of his power, his success, his unwavering ambition. He had built an empire, a network of influence that stretched across continents, a force to be reckoned with. But empires were fragile, built on shifting sands. Loyalty was a currency that could be devalued overnight, trust a commodity that could be shattered in an instant. Christo knew that he could not afford to be complacent, could not allow sentimentality to cloud his judgment. He had made his choice, had drawn a line in the sand. Jax and Big D were on their own. If they succeeded in resolving the crisis in Lubbock, if they managed to salvage their reputation and repay their debts, they would be spared.

But if they failed, they would become another casualty in the ruthless game of power and survival.

Christo stepped out onto the terrace, the warm sun kissing his skin. He gazed out at the endless horizon, his eyes narrowed in contemplation. The future was uncertain, the path ahead fraught with danger. But Christo was not afraid. He had faced challenges before, had overcome obstacles that would have crushed lesser men.

He was a survivor, a master strategist, a ruthless pragmatist. He would navigate the shifting sands, adapt to the changing tides, and emerge victorious. The Cartel would endure, its power undiminished, its influence unchallenged. And Christo, the architect of its success, would find a way to take his rightful spot at the top again and reign supreme. He would ensure it, no matter the cost.

Meanwhile, Jax stared at the phone in his hand, his breaths quick, eyes narrow. Christo's words echoed in his mind, each syllable a hammer blow to his already fractured sense of loyalty. He had given everything to the Cartel, lost his friends, his family, his own peace of mind, all in the name of loyalty, of ambition, of the promise of a better future. But now, that loyalty meant nothing. He was expendable, a pawn to be sacrificed in the name of profit and power. His family, his remaining loved ones, were nothing more than collateral damage, bargaining chips in a game he no longer understood, a game he could no longer win.

He felt nauseous, the taste of bile rising in his throat. He stumbled out of the hospital waiting room, the sterile fluorescent lights blurring into streaks of white and gray. He needed air, needed space, needed to escape the suffocating weight of betrayal and despair that threatened to crush him.

He burst through the hospital doors, the cool night air hitting him like a slap in the face. He gasped for breath, his lungs burning, his heart pounding against his ribs like a trapped bird. He looked up at the star-studded sky, the vast expanse a mocking reminder of his own insignificance, his own powerlessness in the face of forces beyond his control.

He thought of Mecia, lying in that hospital bed, her life hanging in the balance. He thought of Ke', her innocence shattered by the relentless onslaught of tragedy. He thought of Big D, his uncle, his partner in crime, now a fugitive, and the thought of being hunted by the very people he had once trusted.

Defiance surged through him, a spark of resistance igniting in the ashes of his shattered dreams. He wouldn't surrender, wouldn't let them win. He would fight back, would protect his family, would find a way to survive, even if it meant defying the Cartel, even if it meant going against everything he had ever believed in.

He clenched his fists, his knuckles popped, his resolve hardening. He would find a way out of this, a way to reclaim his life, his family, his future. Jax White was not a man to be underestimated. He was a survivor, a fighter, a force to be reckoned with.

Chapter 17
Between Hope and Despair

The sterile fluorescent lights of the hospital waiting room cast a harsh glare on Jax's face, highlighting the exhaustion etched into his features. He slumped in the uncomfortable plastic chair, his phone clutched in his hand, the screen still glowing with notifications of more missed calls and text but Christo's chilling words constantly occupied his attention.

"*Eliminated...*" he muttered, the word a venomous whisper that echoed in the sterile silence of the room. His mind reeled, struggling to process the betrayal, the sudden shift in the sands of loyalty that had once seemed so solid.

He couldn't afford to break down, not now, not when his mother's life hung in the balance, not when Ke' needed him more than ever. Glancing at his sister, curled up on the adjacent chair, her face tear streaked, her eyes closed in a fitful sleep. Jax envied her ability to find even a moment's respite from the relentless onslaught of tragedy that had besieged their family. He wished he could close his eyes and shut out the world, if only for a moment, to escape the suffocating weight of responsibility that pressed down on him.

But there was no escape, not now, not ever. He was Jax, the heir to a legacy of violence and heartbreak. The protector of a family teetering on the brink of destruction. He had to be strong, had to find a way to navigate this treacherous landscape, to shield his sister from the storm that threatened to engulf them all.

The television mounted on the wall caught his eye again, the images a silent montage of chaos and despair. Gabrielle Renee's face filled the screen, her voice a somber counterpoint to the frantic images flashing behind her. Jax watched as she recounted the events of the past few weeks, the tragedies that had befallen his family, the accusations that swirled around them like vultures circling a dying animal.

He saw the footage of the bombed-out police precinct, the charred remains of Kam's car, the tear-streaked faces of his mother and sister. He heard Gabrielle's voice, laced with a mix of empathy and outrage, as she detailed the Cook family's descent into despair, their dreams shattered, their lives irrevocably altered.

And then, the final blow. Gabrielle's voice dropped to a conspiratorial whisper as she revealed the latest twist in the saga – Big D's escape from prison, his alleged involvement in the bombing, his connection to the infamous Corona Cartel. The camera zoomed in on Big D's mugshot, his face a mask of defiance and desperation.

More anger, and primal rage coursed through his veins. He felt as if they were painting him and his family as villains, as criminals, as a threat to the very city they had once called home. It hurt to hear the truth, although some people were twisting the narrative to certain extents.

He wanted to scream, to lash out, to break free from the suffocating web of craziness. But he couldn't. He had to remain calm, maintain his composure, and find a way to sustain the fallout.

The television screen switched to a live feed of the hospital, the camera focused on the entrance. A reporter's voice, breathless and excited, announced the arrival of Detective Crockerette, the lead investigator on the case. Jax watched as Crockerette stepped out of his car, his face grim, his eyes scanning the crowd with a practiced intensity.

Crockerette, the man who was supposed to be his ally, his confidante within the corrupt system was now an enigma. Was he truly on Jax's side, or was he playing a deeper game, his loyalties ultimately lying with the Cartel? Jax couldn't be sure, and that uncertainty gnawed at him, adding another layer of complexity to an already impossible situation.

Jax felt a chill crawl down his spine. He was trapped, surrounded by enemies, with nowhere to turn. The Cartel, the police, the media – they were all closing in, eager to tear him down, to destroy everything he had ever built.

He glanced at Ke', her breathing shallow. He wanted to get her out of here, to find a safe place.

But where could they go? Who could they trust? Their world filled with hidden dangers and shifting alliances. Every step he took could be his last, every decision a potential death sentence.

Time crawled by, each minute an eternity. Jax paced the waiting room restlessly, his mind a whirlwind of conflicting thoughts and emotions. He replayed Christo words in his head, each syllable a fresh wound on his pride, his loyalty, his sense of self.

He thought of his mother, lying unconscious in that hospital bed, her life hanging by a thread. The possibility of her overcoming this blow to her health only to fall victim to the hands of Cartel Hitmen.

Ke', her innocence shattered by the relentless onslaught of tragedy. He thought of Big D, his uncle, his partner in crime, now a fugitive, instead of free with his family.

Finally, after what seemed like an eternity, a doctor emerged from Mecia's room, his expression a mix of weariness and cautious optimism.

"Mr. White," he said, his voice gentle, "Your mother is awake. She's still weak, but she's asking for you."

Jax felt a surge of relief, and gratitude. He thanked the doctor, his voice thick with emotion. He hastily woke his sister and then stepped into Mecia's room, Ke' trailing behind him.

The room was dimly lit, the only source of light a small lamp on the bedside table. Mecia lay propped up in the bed, her breathing shallow. A liquid IV drip snaked into her arm, the clear fluid a lifeline in the fight for her survival.

Jax approached the bed, his footsteps silent on the hard floor. He reached out, his hand hovering over Mecia's frail form.

"Ma," he whispered, his voice thick with emotion. "How are you feeling?"

Mecia's lips curled into a weak smile. "Jax," she rasped, her voice barely above a whisper. "I'm... I'm so tired."

Jax's heart clenched. He could see the weariness in her eyes, the toll that the recent events had taken on her frail body. He knew that her time was running out no matter how bad he wished that wasn't the case.

"Ma," he began, his voice trembling, "Don't talk. Just rest."

But Mecia shook her head. She acknowledged Ke' and took her hand as she came to the empty side of the bed and sat as close as she could for comfort. Then, she set her gaze fixed on Jax with an intensity that rivaled her weakness.

"There's... there's something I need to tell you," she rasped, her voice strained. "But first..." her eyes searched his, a flicker of desperation in their depths. "Where's Jr.? I need to see him. I want to see my grandson. Can you get him here?"

Jax's heart sank. He had been dreading this moment, the moment when he would have to tell his mother the truth about Jr. The truth that had been gnawing at him for days. A truth that had shattered his world and left him feeling even more hollow and broken.

"Ma," he began, his voice cracking, "there's something you need to know about Jr."

Ke' gasped, her eyes widening in alarm. Jax glanced at her, then back to his mother, his heart heavy with the weight of the truth he was about to reveal.

"Cori..." he began, his voice faltering, "She... she took him."

Mecia's eyes widened in disbelief. "Took him?" She echoed, her voice barely a whisper. "What do you mean, took him?" She was appalled.

Jax took a deep breath, steeling himself for the pain he was about to inflict. "She left, Ma," he said, his voice breaking. "She took Jr. and ran away. I don't know where they are, or if I'll ever see him again."

Mecia's face crumpled, tears streaming down her cheeks. Ke' sobbed openly, her body shaking with added grief for her nephew.

Jax felt terrible. His failures as a man and father crushing him. He had failed to protect his son, had failed to keep him safe from the clutches of a woman who had betrayed him in the most cruel and heartless way imaginable. And now, he had to watch as his mother and sister crumbled under the weight of it.

"I'm so sorry, Ma," he whispered, his voice thick with emotion. "I should have protected him. I should have known better than to trust her with him for this long."

Mecia reached out, her trembling hand grasping his. "It's not your fault, Jax," she rasped, her voice weak but firm. "You couldn't have known. None of us could have known."

She paused, her breath coming in ragged gasps. Jax waited, his heart aching, his mind a whirlwind of guilt and regret. "There's... there's something else I need to tell you," Mecia said, her voice barely audible. "...something important."

Jax leaned closer, his heart pounding in his chest. He could sense the urgency in her voice, the weight of unspoken words hanging in the air.

"What is it, Ma?" he asked, his voice barely a whisper.

Mecia's eyes flickered towards Ke', then back to Jax. "I honestly don't feel too good. I've dealt with these bad health issues longer than either of ya'll have walked God's green earth and I've never felt like this. I wish it wasn't so son but I think this may be my last fight. And before I go I have to right a wrong and tell you about your father," he said, her voice barely audible.

"Ma don't say that," Ke' interjected. She couldn't even fathom the thought of her mother not being there anymore. "The Doctors said that you—"

"God is my Doctor and I know what he's saying my child," Mecia cut her off and squeezed her hand tighter. A loving gesture of a mother consoling her young. "I love the both of you dearly, I'm sure you know that."

Jax's breath hitched. He was hurt by the finality in which his mother was speaking. Thoughts of her dying made life seem pointless.

"Before I leave this world I have to tell you son…" Mecia insisted.

Jax's father, the man he had never known, the man who had seemingly abandoned him and his mother before he was even born. The man whose name he had never even spoken.

"Ma," he wiped a tear, his voice thick with emotion, "Why now? Why bring this up now? That nigga don't matter at this point," Jax declared.

Mecia's gaze held his, her eyes filled with a sadness that mirrored his own. "Because it's important," she rasped, her voice growing weaker. "And you deserve to know the truth."

She paused, her breath coming in ragged gasps. Jax waited, his heart pounding, his mind overloaded with questions and anxieties.

"Jax," Mecia began, her voice barely a whisper, "Have ever wondered why your last name isn't Cook?"

Jax frowned, confusion clouding his features. He never really paid attention to his last name and it being different from his mother, brother or sisters. Growing up the man was never mentioned or pictured. In his mind, his father had simply abandoned them. But now, her question planted a seed of doubt in his mind, a suspicion that there was more to the story than he had ever known.

"Momma," he said, his voice laced with uncertainty, "What are you trying to say?"

Mecia's eyes flickered towards Ke' again, then back to Jax. "Your father..." she began, her voice strained, "He didn't abandon you, Jax. I... I pushed him away."

Jax's mind reeled. What was his mother trying to tell him? Who was his father? Why had she kept this secret from him for so long? Why had she pushed his father away? "Okay, tell me the truth. Who was he and why did you do that?"

Mecia took a deep breath, her chest heaving with the effort. "He was... he was someone I loved very much, Jax," she said, her voice gaining strength. "Someone who loved me, too. But our love... it was complicated."

Jax's confusion deepened. Complicated? What did she mean, complicated?

"He was into a lot of shit with your uncle and some other people. Your grandmother and grandfather weren't his biggest fans, Jax," Mecia continued, her voice trembling. He was everything I ever wanted in a man. He was smart, handsome, charismatic, and ambitious. But he was also a product of his environment, a man who had grown up in the streets, a man who had learned to survive by any means necessary." She stared intently at Jax, "And with his lifestyle came other women and that was the root of our issue."

Jax's eyes widened in surprise. That should even have been a surprise. His father, some kinda *street nigga*? It seemed impossible, a contradiction in terms.

He had always imagined his father as a figure. Mecia began to speak in more depth and Jax listened to his mother's words as she painted a picture. A picture of a man who was both alluring and dangerous, a man who had captured her heart but also broke it.

"But why?" Jax pushed. He had to understand. He was a father himself.

"Why did you push him away? Why deny me the chance to know him?"

Mecia's eyes filled with tears. "Because... because I was afraid, Jax," she said, her voice faltering. "Afraid of what he would become, afraid of you becoming just like him."

She paused, her gaze intense, her voice barely a whisper. "And because... because of what I did, Jax. Because of the terrible thing I did to save him."

Jax's heart pounded in his chest. What was she talking about? What terrible thing had she done?

"It all started one day back in 1992 at a United Supermarket, son," Mecia continued, her voice trembling. "I had just left your father's house, and as usual, I went to the store to pick up a few things for grandma and everyone before going home. I was six or seven months pregnant with you at the time."

She closed her eyes, her face contorted in pain as the memories flooded back, vivid and agonizing.

"I was walking down the aisle pushing my basket when I overheard two women talking up in front of me talking a little loud and giggling. And a few of the things they were saying struck me as really familiar. They were talking about your father, about how he had charmed one of them, how he had promised to rock her world."

Mecia's voice cracked with emotion. "I was consumed by jealousy, at that moment. I couldn't bear the thought of him being with someone else, of him betraying me, of him not loving me the way I loved him. Hurt as I was, I continued listening and their conversation took a dark turn. The woman speaking had revealed an unexpected twist - she wasn't just infatuated with Marcellus, nor falling for his advances, but she lucked up and stumbled upon a real opportunity. She intended to rob and and maybe *kill* him in order to prove her loyalty to her true love, a ruthless *Blood Gang* leader named, Ruler Red."

Ke' and Jax were enamored into the story as Mecia told it, nobody noticing her heart rate dropping slowly on the monitor. She continued on telling how she followed the women, her heart pounding in her chest, her mind racing. There was no way these bitches were serious. She knew Mar wouldn't let anything like that happen, but still she trailed them to his house, her every instinct screaming at her to turn back, to run away and remove herself from the situation entirely.

But she couldn't. She had to know, had to see for herself if it was true. And stop it if it was. She crept closer to the house, her senses heightened, her every nerve on high alert. Through the window, she saw them. Marcellus and the woman, locked in a passionate embrace. Mecia's heart shattered, the pain of betrayal a sharp, piercing agony.

But even as the tears streamed down her face, she couldn't shake the feeling that maybe that bitch was seriously gonna try something. The woman's eyes, cold and calculating, held a glint of malice that sent a shiver down Mecia's spine.

Suddenly, the woman reached into her purse, her hand emerging with a gleaming blade. Mecia gasped, her hand flying to her mouth to stifle a scream.

She had to act, had to stop her, had to save Marcellus. Without a second thought, Mecia burst through the door, her eyes wild, her voice a desperate cry. "No!"

The woman whirled around, surprise and anger flashing across her face. But before she could react, Mecia lunged, her hand holding the small weapon Mar himself had given her and insisted she carry in her purse for protection during the time she may be alone during her pregnancy. At first Mecia resisted, raised not to believe in guns and what they represented but Mar's reasoning and insistence won. A single shot rang out, the sound deafening in the confined space. The woman's eyes widened in shock, her body crumpling to the floor, the knife clattering harmlessly away.

Mecia stood frozen, the gun still clutched in her trembling hand, her eyes fixed on the lifeless form at her feet. She had killed a woman, had taken a life to save a life. The weight of her actions crashed down on her, crushing her spirit, shattering her innocence.

Marcellus rushed to her side, his eyes filled with a mixture of horror and gratitude. He held her close, his voice soothing, his touch reassuring, but also infuriating. Even as he comforted her, Mecia couldn't shake the feeling that she had crossed a line, that she had done something unforgivable for her own morals.

The aftermath of that day was a blur of confusion and despair. Mecia was consumed by guilt, haunted by the image of the woman she had killed. She couldn't escape the feeling that she had ruined everything, that she had destroyed her own happiness, her own future.

Chapter 18
The Shadow of Death

The sterile hum of the hospital machinery blended with the hushed whispers of nurses and the distant clatter of medical carts, creating a somber symphony that echoed through the dimly lit corridors. Jax sat beside his mother's bed, his hand clasped tightly around hers, his eyes fixed on her frail form, searching for any sign of change, any flicker of hope in the face of encroaching despair.

The revelation of his father's identity, of his mother's hidden past, of the sacrifices she had made to protect him, had left him reeling, his mind a maelstrom of conflicting emotions. He was angry, confused, and heartbroken, yet also filled with a newfound sense of understanding of his mother's ways, a deeper appreciation for the woman who had shaped his life, who had shielded him from the darkness that threatened to consume them from birth.

But even as he grappled with the weight of these revelations, a more immediate threat loomed. His mother's condition was deteriorating, her body succumbing to the insidious poison that coursed through her veins, her spirit fading with each labored breath.

The news of her poisoning had been a cruel twist of fate, a final blow in a relentless series of tragedies that had befallen his family. He had failed to protect them, had failed to shield them from the violence and betrayal that seemed to follow them like a shadow.

And now, as he watched his mother slip away, he felt a surge of helplessness, a crushing sense of defeat. The darkness had found them, had infiltrated their lives, had poisoned their hearts and minds.

He glanced at Ke', her head resting on the edge of the bed, her eyes locked in on her mother. She had witnessed too much, had endured too much for someone so young. The innocence of her life had been shattered.

Jax needed to protect her and find a way to shield her from the darkness that threatened to consume them all. But how? Where could they go? Who could they trust? The world had become a treacherous landscape, filled with hidden dangers and shifting alliances. Every step he took could be his last, every decision a potential death sentence.

A knock on the door startled him from his reverie. He looked up to see a figure silhouetted against the dim light of the hallway.

"Jax?" a voice inquired, its tone hushed and respectful.

Jax recognized the voice. It was Detective Crockerette, the lead investigator on the case, the man who had once been his ally, his confidante within the corrupt system. But now, Crockerette was an enigma, his motives shrouded in uncertainty, his loyalties unclear.

Jax hesitated, his hand instinctively reaching for the gun tucked into the waistband of his jeans. He couldn't be sure if Crockette was friend or foe, if he had come to offer help or to deliver another blow.

"Come in," Jax said, his voice wary, his eyes fixed on the detective as he stepped into the room.

Crockette's face was grim, his eyes filled with a mixture of concern and apprehension. He glanced at Mecia, her frail form barely visible beneath the white sheets, her breathing shallow and labored.

"I spoke with the Doctors to get some clarity on how this happened. And I may have a lead. How is she?" Crockette inquired, his voice soft.

"Not good," Jax replied, his voice thick with emotion.

Crockette nodded, his gaze lingering on Mecia for a moment before turning back to Jax. "I'm sorry," he said, his voice sincere. "I know this is a difficult time for you and your family."

Jax remained silent, his eyes fixed on the detective, his mind racing. What was Crockette's game? What did he want? He signaled for the man to step out of the room with him into the hall.

"Jax," Crockette began, his voice low and urgent, "We need to talk. Things have changed. The Cartel... they're not happy."

Jax's heart pounded a little in his chest. Crockerette knew.

"They're blaming us, Jax," Crockerette continued, his gaze intense.

"Blaming us for the mess in Lubbock, for the losses, for the bad publicity. They're saying we've become liabilities, that we're jeopardizing their operations."

Jax felt a surge of anger, a bitter taste rising in his throat. "And what do you expect me to do?" he spat, his voice laced with resentment. "I'm the one who is losing damn near everything and everybody. And I still don't know why any of this even started."

Crockette held up his hands, a placating gesture. "I know, Jax. I know it's not fair. But we can't fight them, not alone. They're too powerful, too ruthless. They'll crush us both if we let them."

Jax's mind reeled. Crockette was right. They were both in danger, both expendable in the eyes of the Cartel. They needed to find a way to protect to protect themselves.

"What do you suggest we do?" Jax asked, his voice wary, his eyes searching the detective's face for any sign of deceit.

Crockerette leaned closer, his voice dropping to a conspiratorial whisper. "We need you to do what everyone else is afraid to do. It is the only way to ensure we will be safe."

Jax hesitated, his mind a maelstrom of conflicting thoughts. Could he trust Crockette? Was this a genuine offer, or a trap? He glanced at Mecia, her breathing growing shallower, her face paler with each passing moment. Ke watching in tears. He couldn't afford to hesitate any longer. He had to make a decision, had to choose a path, had to find a way to protect his sister and still be alive to find his son again, but if Detective Crockette hinting at what Jax assumed this would be dangerous and totally immoral and opposites of his beliefs despite the circumstances.

"What do you have in mind?" Jax asked, his voice barely a whisper.

Crockette smiled, a grim satisfaction spreading across his face. "I knew you were a smart man, Jax," he said, his voice laced with a hint of admiration. "I knew you'd see the sense in this."

He leaned closer, his voice dropping to a conspiratorial whisper. "Here's what I propose..."

But as he listened to Crockette's plan, a nagging doubt lingered in the back of his mind. He realized there and then this was all a trap. He knew how the Cartel would play. And this was their play. For the Corona Cartel, Detective Crockette was probably just one of many officers on payroll. He was probably truly expendable and could be easily replaced for the right price, However, Jax on the other hand with the extensive gained revenue and his status within the organization was different.

Jax knew Crockette was playing his part, as he was ordered and he was probably wearing a wire for the Cartel. He understood the detective's fate was probably aligned with his be it good or bad. It was all smoke and mirrors. Even at an inappropriate time like this, they were testing to see if he would fold on them and snitch after they clearly their shoulders on him this time. They would use whatever he said in this moment against him to decide if Jax and his family lived or died.

He glanced at Mecia again peeking through the door, her breathing now shallow and erratic, her body wracked with tremors.

"Look, whoever it is you answer to tell that muthafucka I ain't gonna flip a'ight. I know what's going on right now. I'm fucked up about all this shit but I ain't no snitch. It's all about the money and they got that coming. I'ma pay it, when I do, that's it. But if you want to be on my list of people they need to leave be. I want answers on the shit with my brother, the real answers. I want to know who the fuck did that shit to my sister. And whatever it is about this lead you say you have on someone poisoning my mother! If you can't do that you ain't no use to me either," Jax stated.

The Detective shook his head knowingly respected Jax's words and backed away.

Jax turned back into the room and sat back down next to Ke' and when he did, Mecia's eyes fluttered open, her gaze locking onto Jax's face.

"Jax," she whispered, her voice barely audible. Jax leaned closer, his heart pounding in his chest. "I'm here, Ma," he said, his voice thick with emotion. "I'm here."

"I'm here too, Mama," Ke' said and Mecia's lips curled into a weak smile, her eyes filled with a love that transcended the pain, the fear, the despair.

"I love you, y'all," she whispered, her voice fading with each word. "Protect each other and find my grandson..."

Her grip on his hand tightened, her eyes searching his, a silent plea for him to find strength, to find a way to survive.

"I will, Ma," Jax promised, his voice breaking. "I swear, I'll protect them."

Mecia's smile widened, a flicker of peace settling over her features. And then, with a final sigh, her eyes closed, her grip loosened, her body stilled.

Jax and Ke' watched in horror, their heart shattering into a million pieces, the world collapsing around them. His mother, his rock, his protector, was gone.

The darkness had claimed her, had stolen her away from him, had left him alone and adrift in a sea of grief and despair.

"Ma!" he cried out, his voice raw with anguish. "Ma, no!" He clutched her hand, his fingers digging into her cold, lifeless flesh, his tears falling onto her pale cheeks.

"Ma!" She screamed, her voice filled with a pain that mirrored Jax's own.

She wrapped her arms around Mecia's still body, her sobs echoing through the silent room.

Jax remained frozen, his mind numb, his body heavy with grief. He had failed. He had failed to protect his family, had failed to save his mother. The darkness had won, had claimed another victim, had left him hollow and broken.

The rest of the night and problems that came with their current situation all felt like a blur. The amount of pain and trauma this family was experiencing Jax wished on no one.

PART II

"Rebuild On Solid Ground"

Chapter 19
Solid Ground

Unable to physically attend the funeral of his beloved sister, niece, nephew or friend was a lot on Big D. Still on the run, he was forced into hiding out in the basement of an old house on Angela's family property, not far outside the city but far enough to avoid detection. Over the last week, he managed to get a few accommodations secretly delivered out to them. Amongst the food, clothing and survival goods for three people, Jax sent a sleek webcam setup and tablet so they could still see and be a part of everything.

Jax live streamed the entire ordeal via active aerial drone footage from a remote controlled system he had enabled at a safe distance. Big D, Tina, and Angela watched the proceedings through the clear lens of a webcam, their hearts heavy with grief, their eyes filled with a longing that could not be fulfilled. They had been forced to remain in hiding, their faces plastered on wanted posters, their names whispered in fear and suspicion. The authorities were relentless in their pursuit, their every move racked, their every line of communication in jeopardy of being intercepted. Big D, his face etched with sorrow and frustration, clenched his fists, his knuckles crackled. He yearned to be there, to stand beside his nephew, to offer his support, to share in the collective mourning. But he knew that his presence would only endanger Jax further, would draw unwanted attention, would jeopardize the fragile safety they had managed to carve out in their secluded hideaway. And with that knowledge, he found a measure of solace, by at least being there in spirit.

The savage trio all watched screen of the tablet as a somber hush fell over the sprawling cemetery, the silence broken only by the mournful chirping of cicadas and the rustling of leaves in through the graveyard.

Jax stood at the edge of the freshly dug graves, his shoulders slumped, his eyes fixed on the five mahogany caskets lined up before him. Each casket represented a piece of his heart, a fragment of his soul, ripped away by the relentless tide of violence and betrayal that had swept through his life.

Mecia, his rock, his protector, the woman who had loved him unconditionally, now lay lifeless in a satin-lined coffin, her face serene, her hands clasped peacefully over her chest. The weight of her absence pressed down on him.

Marcus, his brother, his confidante, the young man whose life had been cut short by a sworn protector of the people now rested in eternal slumber, his dreams of athletic glory forever unrealized. The memory of his infectious laughter, his unwavering loyalty, his boundless energy, brought a fresh wave of grief crashing over Jax, a reminder of the irreplaceable bond they had shared.

Kam, his sister, his shining star, the talented artist whose music had touched the hearts of millions, now lay silent, her voice forever silenced by a cowardly act of terror. The thought of her vibrant spirit, her infectious smile, her unwavering determination, brought a lump to Jax's throat, a painful reminder of the light that had been extinguished.

Hot Boi, his homie, a man who had stood by him through thick and, now rested in peace, his life a testament to the unwavering bonds of brotherhood, his death a tragic reminder of the fragility of life. The memory of his unwavering loyalty, his knowledge and energy, brought a tear to Jax's eye, a painful reminder of the friend he had lost.

And Leslie, his business partner, the woman who had believed in him, who made lots of money with him, now lay still. The memory of her sharp wit, her unwavering loyalty, brought a pang of regret to Jax's heart, a reminder of the friend he had failed to protect.

The crowd surrounding the graves was a microcosm of the city, a reflection of the diverse lives that had been touched by these tragedies. Athletes, their heads bowed in respect, mourned the loss of Marcus, their teammate, their friend, their brother in arms. Musicians, their eyes filled with sorrow, paid tribute to Kam, their muse, their inspiration, their voice of a generation. Churchgoers, their hands clasped in prayer, honored Mecia, their pillar of faith, their beacon of hope, their guiding light. And the streets, the hustlers, the survivors, mourned the loss of Leslie and Hot Boi, their comrades, their confidantes, their partners in the struggle.

The service began, the pastor's voice a somber baritone that echoed through the stillness of the cemetery. He spoke of loss, of grief, of the fragility of life, of the enduring power of love and faith. He spoke of the victims, of their dreams, their accomplishments, their legacies. He spoke of the families, of their pain, their resilience, their unwavering hope.

Jax listened to the pastor's words, his heart heavy with grief, his mind a whirlwind of memories and regrets. He thought of all the things he could have done differently, all the choices he had made that had led them to this moment. He thought of his own failures, his own shortcomings, his own inability to protect those he loved. He thought of the darkness that had consumed his life, the violence that had stained his hands, the betrayal that had shattered his trust.

And he thought of the future, the uncertain path that lay ahead, the challenges he would face, the battles he would have to fight. He knew that the road to redemption would be long and arduous, that the scars of the past would never fully heal. But he also knew that he couldn't give up, couldn't surrender to the darkness that threatened to engulf him. He had to find a way to move forward, to rebuild his life, to honor the memory of those he had lost, to protect those who remained.

He glanced at Ke', her tears flowing freely now, her body wracked with sobs. He reached out, his hand gently stroking her hair, his touch a silent promise of comfort and protection. He looked at the crowd behind them, at the many faces etched with grief and sorrow, at the eyes filled with a mixture of anger and despair.

He knew that they were all looking to him, looking for answers, looking for leadership, looking for hope. And in that moment, Jax found his resolve. He would not let them down. He would not let the darkness win. He would rise from the ashes of his shattered dreams, would rebuild his life on solid ground, would forge a new path, a future where his loved ones could live in peace, free from the shadows that had haunted them for far too long or die trying.

Chapter 20
Picking Up the Pieces

As the holidays season neared and the beginning of a new year was on the surfacing, the silence in the sprawling mansion was a suffocating presence, the exact opposite of the vibrant energy that had once pulsed through its veins. 2019 had been a brutal year but would have nothing on the year 2020.

Dust motes danced in the slivers of sunlight that filtered through the heavy drapes, illuminating the emptiness that clung to every corner, every surface, every room. The air was stale, heavy with the scent of neglect and the lingering echoes of laughter and music, now silenced by the cruel hand of fate.

Jax wandered through the vast corridors, his footsteps muffled by the plush carpets, each step a heavy thud against the hollow silence that enveloped him. The mansion, once a symbol of his success, his ambition, his dreams of a future filled with family and friends, now felt like a mausoleum, a monument to the ghosts that haunted its halls.

He paused before a framed photograph on the grand piano, his fingers tracing the outline of his mother's face, her smile frozen in time, her eyes sparkling with a love that death had cruelly extinguished. A wave of grief assaulted him, the pain of her absence a physical ache in his chest, a gaping wound that refused to heal as the days rolled by. He thought of Marcus, his brother, his friend, the young man whose life had been brutally stolen, his dreams of athletic glory forever out of reach. He thought of Kam, his sister, his shining star, her vibrant spirit extinguished, her music silenced by a cowardly act of terror. He thought of Hot Boi and Leslie, their loyal friendship, their unwavering support, now just fading memories, their laughter and smiles lost to the abyss of death.

And he thought of Jr., his son, his precious boy, ripped from his arms by a betrayal that cut deeper than any knife, a wound that festered with guilt and regret. The weight of his grief was almost unbearable, a heavy burden that threatened to buckle his knees, to steal his breath, to extinguish the last embers of hope that flickered within his weary soul. But he couldn't give in, couldn't surrender to the darkness that beckoned him with promises of oblivion. He had to be strong, had to find a way to claw his way back from the precipice, to rebuild his life, to honor the memory of those he had lost, to protect the one precious soul that remained.

He glanced at Ke', curled up on the sofa in the living room, her small frame swallowed by the oversized cushions, her face pale and drawn, her eyes fixed on the muted television screen, the pacing images a meaningless distraction from the pain that gnawed at her heart. She had witnessed too much, had endured too much for someone so young. The innocence of her childhood had been brutally snatched away, replaced by a weariness that aged her beyond her years.

He thought of Big D, his uncle, his partner in crime, now a fugitive, forced to live in the shadows, hunted by the very people he had once trusted. They spoke via webcam every day, their conversations a lifeline in the sea of loneliness and despair that threatened to engulf them. Especially for D and the ladies. They wanted out of that horrid basement but had no choice but to stay put for the foreseeable future.

Although the Cartel accepted Jax's money in exchange for their freedom and release from the coverage of their umbrella, in his mind he couldn't, or shouldn't stay in Lubbock, couldn't risk exposing Ke' to further danger. He wanted to get them both out of the city, to fully escape the clutches of the Cartel, or anyone who may have had a beat on them. But where could they go? Who could they trust? The world had become a treacherous battleground, where every step was fraught with peril, every decision a gamble with their lives.

He thought of his father, Marcellus, the man he had never known, the man whose legacy he now carried within him. He wondered if his father had ever faced similar challenges, had ever felt the same suffocating weight of responsibility, the same crushing burden of grief and loss.

Jax closed his eyes, his mind a maelstrom of conflicting thoughts and emotions. He had to find a way to move forward, to rebuild his life, to protect his family. But how? Where could he start?

A soft knock on the door startled him from his reverie. He looked up to see Ke' standing in the doorway, her eyes filled with a mixture of sadness and determination.

"Jax," she said, her voice soft yet resolute, "I'm going back to school."

Jax's eyebrows rose in surprise. "School?" He echoed, his voice laced with concern. "But Ke', is that safe? With everything that's going on..."

Ke' nodded, her gaze unwavering. "I know it's not ideal, but I can't just stay here and hide. I need to get back to my life, to my friends, to my studies. I need to feel normal again. Alive."

Jax's heart ached for his sister, for the strength and resilience she displayed in the face of such adversity. He knew that she was right. They couldn't let fear cripple them, couldn't let the darkness win. Life, however fragile and unpredictable, had to go on. "Okay, Ke'," he said, his voice filled with a newfound resolve. "You go back to school. I'll take care of everything else."

Ke' smiled, hope shining in her eyes, a spark of the vibrant spirit that had always defined her. "Thank you, brother," she said, her voice filled with gratitude. "I knew you'd understand."

She turned and walked out of the room, her shoulders squared, her head held high, a show of her enduring.

Sadly, Jax watched her go, his heart filled with a mixture of pride and protectiveness. He would do whatever it took to keep her safe.

Since the funeral, he made Ke' go out with him on his property to a shooting range that he had set up. He showed her how to use a weapon to protect herself and turns out although timid at first, she was actually a good shot. The small .380 he made her carry made him feel a little better with her out of his sights.

As he turned his attention back to the daunting task before him, the seemingly insurmountable challenge of rebuilding his life, of reclaiming his future from the wreckage of the past. He had severed ties with the cartel, had paid the exorbitant price for his freedom, had secured the safety of his loved ones. But the battle was far from over.

He had to find Jr., had to bring him home, had to reunite his family, to heal the gaping wound that Cori's betrayal had inflicted. He wanted to reach out to his father, he needed to understand his legacy and to come to terms with the choices that had shaped his life, the forces that had molded him into the man he was today.

Jax took a deep breath, his resolve hardening with each inhale. He would not surrender, would not give up, would not rest until he had achieved his new goals, until he had secured the safety and happiness of his family, until he had found his own redemption, his own sense of peace.

Chapter 21
A Twisted Connection

The insistent buzzing of her phone dragged Ke' from the depths of her day dream. She blinked, her eyes struggling to adjust to the dim light in the classroom she was in. Groaning, she reached for the device, her fingers fumbling across the her desk.

She unlocked the phone with her fingerprint and the bright light lit up. A text message from an unsaved number appeared. Curiosity piqued, she swiped the screen up, her eyes scanning the message:

"Hey, Ke'. It's TJ. I know things have been rough lately, and I just wanted to check on you. Hope you're doing okay. ☺ "

TJ? The name stirred her memory, a fleeting image of a kind face. He had been one of Jax's friends, a fellow musician along with her sister, Kam on the Hub City Records Label.

She typed a quick reply, her fingers trembling slightly. "Hey, TJ. Thanks for checking on me. I'm... I'm doing okay, I guess. Just trying to get through each day." She hesitated, then added: "It's hard to focus now without Kam, Marcus or my mom. I miss them so much!"

A tear slipped down her cheek, the salty taste a bitter reminder of her loss. She quickly wiped it away, not wanting to give in to the negative emotion that threatened to consume her. Or for any classmates to notice. She tried to give her attention back to the professor and his lesson but almost instantly, her phone buzzed again.

"I know it is. Your mother was a really sweet lady. Marcus was a cool kid and hell of a player. And Kam was an amazing person. She touched so many lives with her music. She may not have been my biggest fan but shit for what it's worth, I miss her too," Terry gamed with his reply.

Ke' felt a warmth spread through her chest, a notion of comfort in the face of overwhelming grief. TJ's words, simple yet sincere, resonated with her, offering a sense of connection, a shared understanding of the pain that gnawed at her soul.

They exchanged a few more messages, TJ's words a soothing balm on her wounded spirit. He was kind, compassionate, and surprisingly funny, his messages peppered with emojis and lighthearted jokes that brought a rare smile to Ke's face.

He asked about her day, about her plans, about her dreams for the future. He listened patiently as she poured out her heart, sharing her fears, her anxieties, her uncertainties about the path that lay ahead.

Soon the days turned into weeks, their connection deepened, their conversations growing more intimate, more personal. Ke' found herself looking forward to his messages, his virtual presence a comforting constant in the chaotic, lonely landscape of her life.

One afternoon, TJ suggested they meet up, just to hang out, to talk, to escape the confines of their grief-stricken homes. Ke' hesitated, her instincts warning her against trusting a stranger, against venturing out into the world that had brought her so much pain. She knew Jax wouldn't agree, but TJ's persistence, his gentle reassurance, and the undeniable allure of his virtual persona, wore down her defenses. She agreed to meet him, choosing a quiet park on the outskirts of town, a place where they could talk without fear of being overheard, without the prying eyes of the media that seemed to follow her every move when they had the opportunity.

The day of their meeting arrived, and Ke' found herself filled with a mixture of excitement and trepidation. She dressed carefully, choosing an outfit that was both comfortable and stylish, wanting to make a good impression, wanting to feel a sense of normalcy, a sense of hope for the future.

She arrived at the park early, her heart pounding in her chest, her palms sweating. She scanned the surroundings, her eyes searching for any sign of TJ, her mind replaying their conversations, wondering if he would be as kind and charming as she believed he was.

And then she saw him, leaning against a tree, his face illuminated by the soft glow of the afternoon sun. He was even more handsome in person then the last time she saw him. His smile warm and inviting, his eyes sparkling with a genuine kindness that melted Ke's anxieties away.

They spent the afternoon talking, laughing, sharing stories, and dreams, and fears. Ke' felt a connection with TJ that she had never experienced before, a sense of understanding, of acceptance, of belonging. He listened to her without judgment, offering words of comfort and encouragement, reminding her of her strength, her resilience, her potential for a brighter future.

As the sun began to set, casting long shadows across the park, TJ reached out, his hand gently touching Ke's arm. "Ke'," he said, his voice soft, "I know things have been tough for you lately. But I want you to know that you're not alone. I'm here for you, and I'll always be here for you if you let me."

Ke's eyes filled with tears, her heart swelling with gratitude. She had found a friend, a confidante, a source of strength in the midst of her despair. She leaned into TJ's embrace, his arms a safe haven, his touch a promise of comfort and support.

As they walked back to Ke's car, hand in hand, the world seemed a little less bleak, the future a little less uncertain. Ke' knew that the road ahead would be long and arduous, filled with challenges and obstacles. But she also knew that she wasn't alone. She had TJ, her new friend, her source of strength.

Meanwhile, Jax was trying to recover and maintain a semblance of normalcy remained oblivious to his sister's budding relationship. He was lost in his own world of grief. Some good days out numbered by the bad ones. His days a blur of numbness, his nights a restless torment of nightmares and regrets. Most days when he just couldn't find peace, he found himself lost in a bottle. The burning alcohol the only fuel that could propel him forward.

He had severed ties with the cartel, had paid the exorbitant price for his freedom, had secured the safety of his loved ones. But that small victory felt hollow, the future uncertain. He had lost so much, had sacrificed so much, and for what? Everybody dealt with trauma differently and he chose his way to cope.

Chapter 22
Unexpected Encounters

One random Saturday, in the middle of January, Jax home alone decided he'd had enough of being inside and made plans to get out for a little bit. Ke' was out with a friend she said and would be in late. He still wasn't himself, but he felt that in order to heal he had to get out of his comfort zone. Lubbock was still his city, he still had friends and fans so why hold himself to this low point.

He got dressed. Nothing too fancy or over the top, No shiny jewelry or big brand items. Just casual attire. But even in that sense he would still outshine most on their best day. He wrestled over the idea of which car of the many he should use, ultimately ending up in his Tesla. He knew in the back of his mind of his intended destination. And if the night went how his usually did, he knew he'd probably need a safe ride home.

***

The dimly lit bar hummed with a low-key energy, a refuge from the biting chill of the late night winter winds in Texas. The scent of stale beer and cigarette smoke hung heavy in the air, mingling with the faint aroma of fried food wafting from the kitchen. A jukebox in the corner crooned a mournful blues tune, its melancholic melody a fitting soundtrack to the somber atmosphere.

107

Jax sat on a barstool, his shoulders slumped, his eyes glazed with a mixture of weariness. He nursed a glass of amber liquid, the ice clinking softly against the rim, the alcohol a temporary anesthetic to the pain that gnawed at his soul. He had ventured out into the city on a whim, seeking a distraction from the suffocating silence of the mansion, the haunting memories that clung to its walls like cobwebs. He had no real purpose other than to escape the ghosts that haunted his waking hours, the nightmares that plagued his sleep.

He had ended up at this nondescript bar, a hole-in-the-wall establishment tucked away in a forgotten corner of the city, its anonymity a welcome respite from the prying eyes of the media, the whispers of gossip and speculation that followed him like a shadow now days. He used to have such an attractive aura and was a people person. But ever since the tragedies started and the story broke it seemed as if people quickly withdrew from him. Avoiding contact because it was believed

Jax's presence brung death to those around him. He ordered a drink and the familiar burn of the whiskey a momentary comfort, a fleeting escape from the crushing weight of his grief. He closed his eyes, letting the music soothe him, the mournful melody a reflection of his own troubled soul.

He thought of Mecia, her gentle smile, her unwavering love, now just a fading memory, a ghost that haunted his dreams. He thought of Marcus and Kam, their vibrant spirits extinguished, their laughter silenced by the cruel hand of fate.

He thought of Hot Boi and Leslie, their loyal friendship, their unwavering support, now just echoes in the empty chambers of his heart.

And he thought of Jr., his son, the boy who had been stolen from him, the boy he longed to hold in his arms again.

The pain of Jr.'s absence was a constant ache, a gaping wound that refused to heal.

He had failed them all. He was a failure, a fraud, a shadow of the man he had once aspired to be. He lifted his glass to his lips, the amber liquid swirling, the ice clinking a rhythmic counterpoint to the bluesy tune. As he took a sip, a figure slid onto the barstool beside him.

Jax glanced sideways, his gaze meeting the eyes of the woman who had settled next to him. Already buzzed a bit, he recognized her vaguely. She was the reporter, the one who had chronicled his family's tragedies with a mix of empathy and condemnation.

He frowned, a jolt of annoyance crossing his features. He wasn't in the mood for questions, for prying eyes, or the relentless scrutiny. He turned away, his gaze returning to the swirling contents of his glass pretending he didn't notice her. He hoped she would take the hint and leave him alone. But she didn't.

"Jaxson?" She asked, her voice soft, hesitant.

He looked at her again, his eyebrows raised in surprise. The way she said his name was as if she actually knew him.

"It's me," she continued, her voice gaining confidence, "Gabrielle."

Jax's mind reeled. Gabrielle? He knew that of course from the news, her face struck

familiar. He searched his memory, trying to place her, then it hit him. "Gabrielle?" He echoed, his voice filled with disbelief. "Gabrielle Aguilara?"

The woman smiled, a warmth spreading across her features. "The one and only," she said, her voice laced with a hint of amusement.

Jax stared at her, his mind racing. Gabrielle Aguilara, the quiet girl from his high school writing class. They partnered up from time to time on different assignments. She was also the one he'd rescued from a disastrous situation at a party years ago. He couldn't believe it. It really was a small world.

Gabrielle Aguilara, an old friend of sorts, the woman whose face had become synonymous with his family's tragedies, was sitting beside him, in this dimly lit bar, as if by some strange twist of fate.

"But... but you're Gabrielle Renee," he stammered, his voice laced with confusion. "The reporter."

Gabrielle chuckled lightly. "That's my professional name," she explained. "Gabrielle Renee. It has a better ring to it for TV, don't you think?"

Jax nodded, his mind still struggling to reconcile the image of the shy, vulnerable girl he had known with the confident, successful woman sitting beside him.

"You look a little different, I... I didn't recognize you," he admitted, his voice filled with a mixture of embarrassment and awe.

Gabrielle's smile softened. "I've changed a bit since high school," she said, her eyes twinkling. "Changed my hair and lost the braces. But you... you haven't changed at all, Jax. You're still the same kind, caring man who saved me that night." She gave him a knowing look.

Jax's heart ached at her words, a reminder of a time when he had been capable of kindness, of compassion, of protecting those who were vulnerable.

"I... I don't know about that," he mumbled, his gaze dropping to his drink.

Gabrielle reached out, her hand gently touching his arm. "Don't sell yourself short, Jax," she said, her voice firm. "You've been through a lot, but you're still a good man. I know it. Right now, it looks like you need someone to talk to."

Jax looked at her, his eyes searching hers for any sign of deceit, any hint of pity. Wondering if she was approaching him for a story angle or legit engagement of some other purpose. But all he saw was sincerity, a genuine belief in him that he dared to believe in himself.

He felt a surge of emotion, maybe it was the liquor or their strange ties. He wanted to confide in her and to unburden his soul. But the words wouldn't come. He was afraid of what she might think, afraid of her judgment, afraid of her rejection. He looked away, his gaze returning to the swirling contents of his glass.

The silence stretched between them, heavy with unspoken words, with the weight of their shared history and with the knowledge of where their lives were now.

The jukebox clicked and sputtered, the bluesy tune fading into silence. A new song began, its upbeat tempo a jarring contrast to the somber atmosphere.

Jax took another sip of his drink, the alcohol burning a path down his throat, a temporary distraction from the turmoil within him. He glanced at Gabrielle again, her gaze fixed on the dance floor, a touch of sadness in her eyes.

He wondered what she was thinking, what she was feeling. Did she see him as a villain, a criminal? Or did she see something more, something beneath the surface, something worth saving? He didn't know. And in that moment, as the music swelled and the dancers twirled, a memory flickered to life in the recesses of his mind.

***

The party pulsed with frenetic energy, the air thick with the scent of sweat, cheap cologne, and spilled liquor. Bodies gyrated on the dance floor, their movements a blur of limbs and flashing lights. Music blared from oversized speakers, the bass vibrating through the floor, through the walls, through Jax's very bones.

Gabrielle had arrived alone, dressed to impress in a tight-fitting dress that hugged her budding curves. It was her first real party, her first time truly indulging in alcohol and unchaperoned teen night life. Only problem was unlike most girls in her class, she didn't have many close friends. But she didn't let that fact keep her inside any longer. She wanted to live.

The spiked punch was deceptively sweet, and she hadn't realized how strong it was until her head began to spin, the world tilting on its axis.

She found a quiet corner, hoping to regain her composure, but a guy named Greg, who had been eyeing her since she walked in, saw his opportunity. He approached her, his smile charming, his words flattering. He made her laugh, made her feel at ease and wanted. Made her forget her natural anxieties.

However, in the midst of their conversation, he "accidentally" spilled his drink on her dress. He apologized profusely, offering to help her clean up in the bathroom upstairs. Gabrielle, her judgment clouded by the alcohol, agreed, allowing him to lead her up the stairs, into a guest bedroom.

Once inside, Greg shut the door and fumbled with the bathroom doorknob, saying it was stuck. Gabrielle, her head spinning, simply flopped onto the bed, needing a moment to rest, to regain her bearings. But Greg had other plans.

He slipped out of the room, returning moments later with two of his friends. They had been promised a "gang bang" with a drunk girl, and they were eager to collect.

They locked the door behind them, their eyes gleaming with predatory hunger. Gabrielle, oblivious to the danger, lay on the bed, her dress slightly askew, her defenses lowered. The men advanced, their hands reaching for her, their words crude and suggestive. Gabrielle, her senses dulled by the alcohol, tried to protest, to push them away, but her efforts were weak, her voice slurred.

One of the men had already lifted her dress, his hand reaching for her panties, when the bathroom door in the room swung open. Jax emerged, his face a mask of confusion, his eyes widening in alarm as he took in the scene before him.

"What the fuck y'all doing?" he roared, his voice filled with rage.

The men turned, startled by the interruption. Gabrielle, seizing the opportunity, kicked and screamed, her cries for help echoing through the room. Jax recognized her instantly. Her eyes filled with a mixture of intelligence and vulnerability.

He felt a surge of protectiveness, a primal urge to defend her from these predators. He lunged forward, his fists flying, his rage fueling his every move. He knocked Greg to the ground with a single punch, then turned on the other two men, his fury a whirlwind of fists and feet. The other men quickly retreated, leaving Gabrielle sobbing on the bed, her dress disheveled, her dignity violated.

Jax knelt beside her, his voice gentle, his touch reassuring. "It's okay, Gabrielle," he whispered. "I'm here now. You're safe." He helped her to her feet, his arm supporting her trembling body. He led her out of the house, ignoring the curious stares and whispers that followed them. He got her into his car, strapped her into the passenger seat, and drove her home.

As they drove, Gabrielle's sobs subsided, replaced by a quiet gratitude. She thanked Jax for his kindness, for his protection, for seeing her, for recognizing her vulnerability. And in that moment, as he looked at her, at the tears glistening in her eyes, at the gratitude shining through her pain, Jax felt a connection with Gabrielle, a connection that transcended as a result of this encounter at the party.

He had saved her that night, had rescued her from a situation that could have turned tragic. And in doing so, he had unknowingly forged a bond that with her that would really come in handy one day.

But the story didn't end there. As they passed through the crowd of partygoers that night, a messy friend of Cori's, a girl named Bria, snapped a picture of Jax and Gabrielle with her phone. She sent the picture to Cori, with no context, no explanation. Just a picture of Jax, holding Gabrielle close, their faces illuminated by the flashing lights of the party.

When she finally made it to the party, Cori was consumed by jealousy and rage. She stormed into the party, her eyes searching for Jax, her heart filled with a desire for revenge. Realizing he wasn't there she assumed the worst case scenario because of the pic and she dove off the deep end. The next move she made then created some of the current chaos. She wanted to show Jax two could play the game but only one could win.

Cori scanned the crowd of men and made a selection. She approached Bundle, her footsteps silent, her anger simmering. She tapped him on the shoulder, and when he turned around, she laid the biggest, wettest kiss on him, a kiss that was both a challenge and a betrayal. Then she unknowingly lead Bundle up stairs to the same room where Jax just had the previous encounter.

***

The memory faded. He looked at Gabrielle, her presence a reminder of a time when he had been capable of kindness, of compassion, of protecting those who were vulnerable. He wondered if she was thinking about that night.

He opened his mouth to speak, but the words still caught in his throat. What could he say? How could he bridge the chasm that separated them? He looked away, his gaze returning to the swirling contents of his glass. The silence stretched between them, heavy with unspoken words.

The jukebox clicked and timed out, the bluesy tune fading into eerie silence. A new song began, its upbeat tempo a jarring contrast to the somber atmosphere.

Jax took another sip of his drink, the alcohol burning a path down his throat. He glanced at Gabrielle again, her gaze fixed on the dance floor. He wondered what she was thinking. They hadn't ever had much of a connection despite that pivotal moment. What was she truly after here? He didn't know. Jax was tired of fighting, tired of running, tired of pretending. He just wanted to be left alone, to drown his sorrows in the anonymity of this dimly lit bar, to forget about all the things he couldn't change. Even if only for a moment. But fate, it seemed, had other plans it seemed.

"What's a girl like you doing in a place like this?" he finally asked, his voice rough.

Gabrielle's lips curved into a wry smile. "Funny you should ask that," she said, her voice low and private. "I'm here for you, Jax."

Jax's eyebrows shot up in surprise. "For me?" he echoed, his voice laced with disbelief. "Why?"

"Because I owe you one," Gabrielle replied, her gaze steady. "And because I think you might need my help."

Jax's heart pounded in his chest. "I don't understand," he said, his voice filled with confusion.

Gabrielle leaned closer, her voice dropping to a whisper. "I know things, Jax. A lot of things," she said, her eyes gleaming with a mix of determination and empathy. "Things that could help you. Things that will sober you right up."

Jax stared at her, his mind reeling. What could she possibly know that could help him? "What are you talking about?" He asked.

Gabrielle's smile faded, her expression turning serious. She reached into the purse beside her and pulled out a thick manila envelope. "I've been doing some digging, Jax," she said, her voice low. "About Marcus."

Jax's heart clenched. Marcus. The pain of his loss was still a raw wound, a constant ache in his chest. He looked at the envelope, his curiosity piqued. What could Gabrielle possibly have found out about Marcus? "What is it?" he asked nervously.

Gabrielle opened the envelope and pulled out a stack of papers. "These are the police files on Marcus's case," she explained. "The official reports, the witness statements, the forensic evidence."

Jax's brow furrowed. "And?"

Gabrielle's eyes got tight. She meant business now "And there's one big hole, Jax. An inconsistent, contradicting, outright lie. Right here in black and white."

She had his attention now. What was she talking about?

Gabrielle pointed to a page in the file. "We all know that Marcus was killed by Detective Sullivan during the traffic stop," she said, her voice filled with controlled anger. "They claim that Marcus was a suspect in the double homicides of Greedy B and D-Lee, who were friends of yours. They claim that he had the murder weapon in his possession."

Jax nodded grimly. He knew the official story. It was the story that had been plastered across the news that had painted his brother as a murderer, a trait that ran in his family lineage.

"But it's not true, Jax," Gabrielle insisted, her voice rising with conviction. "I know Marcus didn't kill anyone. He was set up." Gabrielle continued, her voice urgent. "I've been looking into the details, Jax. The timeline, the evidence, the witness statements. And I've found something that doesn't add up."

She paused, her gaze holding his. "Marcus couldn't have killed Greedy and D-Lee, Jax. He was somewhere else at the time."

Jax's look was intent. He knew this was true but couldn't prove it, how could she? And if she could obtain the knowledge of Marcus' innocence so firmly, how come the police couldn't? What the fuck was really going on?

Gabrielle smiled, a triumphant glint in her eyes. "He was at home, Jax. Playing video games."

Jax's eyebrows shot up in surprise. "Video games?"

Gabrielle nodded. "Remember that app, Review The Footage? The one that records you while you watch game film?"

Jax nodded. He remembered. It was an app that a lot of the athletes used, including Marcus.

"Well, I checked his account, Jax," Gabrielle explained. "And guess what? He logged in that night. The night of the murders. And he watched film for hours. There's a video record of it, Jax and in that video it shows Marcus sitting in his room in a game chair playing a video game while simultaneously watching film tutorials. He couldn't have been anywhere else."

Could this be true? Could Gabrielle have found the evidence that would clear his brother's name? "But why?" he asked, "Why would anyone set him up?"

Gabrielle's smile faded, her expression turning grim again. "I don't know for sure, Jax," she admitted. "But I have a theory." She leaned closer, "I think it has something to do with Detective Sullivan and your families history on a personal level."

"What do you mean personal?" Jax asked, his voice laced with suspicion.

Gabrielle's gaze hardened. "Okay, this may sound crazy but I've done a lot of digging and I think it makes sense. Basically Jax, I think Detective Sullivan has had a hand in the troubles that have recently surrounded you. I think he's had it out for your uncle for many years and by retaliating against him has created this domino effect of tragedy."

This was heavy to process but being directly at the center of it all Jax had a feeling she wasn't far off the truth. As she carried on, he began to see things in the full scope.

"Back in 2003 when your uncle was sentenced to life in prison for his alleged crimes, he had one of the most infamous courtroom outbursts ever and savagely murdered multiple people including his lawyer, a testifying FBI witness and the Judge. As we both know, the world is small and Lubbock is even smaller. That very judge just so happened to be Detective Sullivan's wife. Now I'm no lawyer, but in hindsight I can see how that connection alone, the sentencing judge being the wife of the charging Detective is unethical and probably illegal, but somehow those details amongst others were looked over. Anyway, from the looks of things it seems that fate put Detective Sullivan in a position where he found himself in position to get an eye for an eye and he did."

Jax didn't know how to respond to this. Shit was deep. Then she went deeper. And what she said made Jax realize just how fucked up his situation was.

"So, knowing all that now made me look at this situation from a different perspective. If Detective Sullivan truly Marcus based solely off revenge, why did he select Marcus? I wondered. In all of the statement information and background we can find on your family, I can see clearly Marcus or your sisters never had a connection to your uncle. He and your mother had their issues, so that leaves you. Now just think for a second, on record out of your whole family, you have the biggest connection to him. So, from the outside looking if someone wanted to take out the closest to your uncle," She let that hint linger in the air before continuing to paint her picture. "That would have been you. But since it wasn't and there's clearly something going on here. It makes me look at this even deeper. Especially with everything else that's happened. From your friends' murder, to Kam's death and even whispers of your mother being poisoned. Factoring it all in, in my eyes it looks like all this was an attack actually directed towards hurting you or bringing you down. The question is why? The only one who can have that answer is you and the only person who has knowledge on those responsible or can be implicated in these terrible crimes is Detective Suillivan and Jax, I hate to lay so much on you but I'm afraid he's in the wind. Hasn't been seen or heard from in weeks. Just gone completely off the grid. There's so many moving parts here it's a bit overwhelming," Gabrielle admitted.

"So, basically you're telling me, you think my friends and family were killed because of me?" Jax asked a little harshly. Hearing shit like that hurt.

"In short, yes. Not that I want it to be true though. It's just everything from a large scope seems more suited to you. If it was about revenge against your uncle, why did your friends die first? Why Marcus, then Kam & your mother. That's way over the top, don't ya think? You're the common denominator in all that, it affects your uncle as well but not as much as you. If it was solely about your uncle I don't see how things would have gotten this deep. I've done many stories over my career in journalism and investigative reporting but nothing touches the surface of this. There's something here," she said, oozing confidence.

As Jax swallowed the last of his drink, he thought long and hard about all that was said, all that was known and contemplated on where to go from there. The rest of their conversations only got deeper.

***

Terry lay sprawled on the bed, his phone clutched in his hand, a triumphant smirk playing on his lips. He scrolled through the latest news reports, his eyes gleaming with a mixture of satisfaction and anticipation. The headlines screamed of Jax's downfall, of his family's tragedies, of his crumbling empire. Each story was a testament to his success, a validation of his twisted plan for revenge.

He thought back to the night he and Tory had killed Kam, the explosion that had further shattered Jax's world, the pain that had ripped through his family. It had been a brutal act, a cold-blooded execution, but Terry felt no remorse. He had done what he had to do, had avenged his brother's death and upped the score.

Now, he was ready for the next phase of his plan. He would continue to torment Jax, would chip away at his sanity, would destroy everything he held dear. He would make him suffer, would make him pay for the sins of his past.

But first, he had to take care of some unfinished business. He had already set the wheels in motion. It was only a matter of time before he revealed the truth, before he brought the whole house of cards crashing down.

Terry had prepared for everything. He would use Jax's last weakness to his advantage. And then, he would watch him crumble, would savor his despair, would revel in his downfall. He would be the architect of Jax's destruction, the author of his final chapter.

But for now, he had other matters to attend to. He had a date with Ke', Jax's little sister, the innocent pawn in his twisted game. He had been grooming her for weeks, showering her with attention, with affection, with the kind of love and support she craved in the wake of her family's tragedies.

He had played the role of the perfect boyfriend, the knight in shining armor who had come to rescue her from her despair. He had listened to her woes, had offered her comfort, had filled the void left by her mother, brother and sister's deaths. And Ke', blinded by her grief, by her loneliness, by her desperate need for connection, had fallen for his charade. She had no idea who he truly was, what his real intentions were or the kind of darkness that lurked beneath his charming facade.

Tonight, they would take their relationship to the next level. He would seduce her, would use her body to fuel his twisted desires, would exploit her vulnerability to further his own agenda.

He glanced at the clock on the nightstand. It was almost time. He rose from the bed, his movements fluid and predatory, his eyes gleaming with anticipation.

He showered, shaved, and dressed in his finest clothes, wanting to look his best for Ke', wanting to impress her, to seduce her, to conquer her.

He checked his phone again, a message from Ke' flashing on the screen. She was on her way. A smile spread across his face, a cruel, predatory smile that revealed the true nature of his intentions. He waited, his patience wearing thin, his desire growing stronger with each passing minute. And then, he heard a knock on the door.

He opened it, his smile widening as hc saw Ke' standing in the doorway, her eyes shining with excitement, her cheeks flushed.

"Hey, beautiful," he said, his voice smooth and seductive. "Come on in."

Ke' stepped into the room, her gaze sweeping over the dimly lit space, her senses filled with the familiar scent of Terry's cologne, the faint aroma of weed and the underlying musk of desire.

Terry closed the door behind her, his eyes locking onto hers, his smile widening. "You look amazing," he said.

Ke' blushed, her heart fluttering in her chest. She had never felt this way about anyone before, this mix of excitement and nervousness, this overwhelming attraction that threatened to consume her.

Terry reached out, his hand gently cupping her cheek, his touch sending shivers down her spine. "I've been looking forward to this all day," he whispered, his voice husky.

Ke' leaned into his touch, her eyes closing as she savored the warmth of his hand, the intimacy of his gaze. She had found solace in his arms, a refuge from the storm that had ravaged her life. He pulled her closer, his lips finding hers in a passionate kiss that ignited a fire within her soul. Ke' responded eagerly, her arms wrapping around his neck, her body pressing against his, her desire mirroring his own.

They fell onto the bed, stripping, their clothes a tangled mess, their bodies entwined in a dance of passion and surrender. The music from the small radio on the nightstand filled the room, the lyrics of Jhene Aiko's "Pussy Fairy" echoing Ke's every move.

"I know you love fuckin' me
I can tell by the way you in love with me
You can't get enough of me, Yeah
Well I guess it's looking like you stuck with me..."

Terry's hands roamed over Ke's body, exploring her curves, igniting a fire within her that she had never known before. Ke' moaned, her senses overwhelmed by the sensations, the pleasure, the surrender.

"'Cause I got you sprung off in the springtime
Fuck all your free time
You don't need no me time
That's you and me time..."

Their bodies moved in sync with the music, their rhythm a primal dance of love and lust, of dominance and submission. Ke' lost herself in the moment, her inhibitions fading, her fears forgotten.

"We be gettin' so loud
That dick make my sole smile
That dick make me so damn proud..."

Terry whispered words of love and encouragement, his voice a seductive melody that lulled Ke' into a state of blissful oblivion. She had found her escape, her release, her salvation in his arms.

"Now lay your head down on the pillow
Turn the lights down real low
I want you to say my name
Close your eyes and let your feels go
Now you're gettin' real close
Baby, I am on the way..."

As the song reached its climax, their bodies reached a crescendo, their passion exploding in a symphony of moans and gasps. Ke' clung to Terry, her heart pounding, her body trembling, her soul soaring.

She had found her haven, her refuge, her love in the arms of a man who would ultimately betray her, who would use her, who would discard her like a broken toy. But at this moment, she was clueless. She was lost in the ecstasy of their embrace, blinded by the illusion of love. Later on down the road life, if it was one thing Ke' wished she could ever take back it would be this particular moment.

Chapter 23
Stay Schemin'

Tory moved out of the way and Terry leaned over the pool table and focused on his shot as the beat in the speaker system built up behind him. A slow ominous sound that weirdly enhanced the overall vibe and set the tone for his match.

Eee err… eee err… eee err…eee err

Terry looked up at his twin as she nodded her head to the beat. She was full of confidence in her game. Had got some lucky shots but he was about to close things out.

Eee err…eee err…eee err
Pullin' out the coupe at the lot,
Told 'em fuck 12, fuck SWAT
Bustin' all the bells out the box
I just hit a lick with the box,
Had to put the stick in the box, Mm
Pour up the whole damn seal,
I'ma get lazy
I got the mojo deals,
We been trappin' like the 80's

He drew back quickly and with light touch and precision thrust his stick forward tapping the cue ball with surprising force. It danced around the blocking eight ball took a unique curve and rolled to knock in his last solid. The table was clear now save for the eight ball. One more shot and he had this win in the bag. He looked up at Tory and winked. She gritted her teeth and tightened the grip on her pool stick praying he missed.

She sucked a nigga soul, gotta CashApp
Told'em wipe a nigga nose, say slatt, slatt
I won't never sell my soul, and I can back that
And I really wanna know where you at, at

He swung around the table lining up for the kill. He found his angle and wasted no time to think. He posed, charged up and shot.

I was out back where the stash at
Cruised the city in a bulletproof Cadillac
'Cause I know niggas after where the bag at
Gotta move smarter, gotta move harder

The cue ball rolled straight-ahead spot-on target but with a bit too much force. It slapped the eight ball with a nice clack that brung the two balls together like magnets and together they rolled into the bottom corner pocket of the table.

Tory broke out in a relentless laughing victory enjoying the moment and the thrill. Right there in something so simple, the universe showed Terry sometimes even when you win, you lose. Taking the overconfident in some cases approach could be the end. But he never thought that deep.

Tory's laughter echoed through the room, bouncing off the walls and mingling with the fading beat of the music.

"Oh my god, Terry! You choked!" she shrieked, wiping a tear from her eye. "Mr. 'I'm about to close things out,' Mr. 'One more shot and I have this win in the bag'!" She mimicked his earlier swagger, exaggerating his stance and winking dramatically. "What happened to all that confidence?"

Terry chuckled, though a bit sheepishly. "Alright, alright, you got me," he admitted, racking the balls for another game. "Guess I got a little too cocky. Beginner's luck, right?" He winked, trying to regain his composure.

"Beginner's luck?" Tory scoffed, grabbing her cue. "Please. I'm a pool shark in disguise. You just unleashed my inner predator." She leaned in close, lowering her voice conspiratorially. "Besides," she added with a sly grin, "Someone has to keep you humble."

"Yeah, yeah," Terry said, rolling his eyes playfully. "Just don't let it go to your head."

Since Kam's hit, life had taken a decidedly different turn for the twins. The initial shock and paranoia had slowly given way to a strange sense of liberation. They'd used a portion of their ill-gotten gains to upgrade their living situation, trading their cramped apartment for a spacious two-story house in a quiet neighborhood. They'd splurged on new clothes, electronics, and even a few frivolous luxuries they'd only dreamed of before. They'd become connoisseurs of takeout, indulging in expensive meals they couldn't pronounce the names of. It was a whirlwind of newfound freedom and indulgence, a stark contrast to the lives they'd led before.

But beneath the surface of carefree living, their shared secret had forged an unbreakable bond. They understood each other in a way no one else could, their shared experience creating a silent pact that transcended words. They'd reveled in the news coverage of Kam's disappearance, following every update with a mixture of excitement and morbid fascination. The police were baffled, the public was intrigued, and Terry and Tory were living their best lives, all while remaining completely anonymous. They were ghosts in the machine, enjoying the spoils of their actions while the world remained clueless.

One evening, as they relaxed on their plush new couch, sipping champagne and watching a movie, Terry turned to Tory, a serious expression on his face.

"Tory," he began, his voice low, "I've moved on to phase two."

Tory raised an eyebrow, intrigued. "Hell yeah, phase two! Wait, what's phase two?"

Terry leaned back, a glint in his eyes. "Remember what we talked about?

This was just the beginning. A steppingstone. I've been working behind the scenes, making connections, laying the groundwork. In about six to eight weeks," he paused, a slow smile spreading across his face, "We'll be ready for the finale just when he thought it was over.

Chapter 24
Morning Sickness

Jax meticulously reviewed the files spread across his dining room table. Eight weeks. Eight weeks since their lives had been irrevocably altered. Eight weeks of clandestine meetings with Gabrielle Renee, piecing together the fragments of what had transpired, sifting through the lies and half-truths to uncover the real story. Gabrielle, a tenacious journalist with a nose for the truth, had become an unlikely ally. She was driven by a thirst for justice, and Jax, by a need to understand.

He rubbed his tired eyes, the weight of the past weeks pressing down on him. He'd walked a tightrope, balancing his burgeoning relationship with Ke' with the ever-present feeling that something was…off. Their moments of normalcy were fleeting, stolen in between the chaos. They'd tried to build a life amidst the wreckage, finding solace in each other's arms, but an unspoken tension lingered, a constant reminder of the darkness that surrounded them.

Ke' was different now. More reserved, more careful. The carefree spirit he'd known for was still there, but it was tempered by a newfound seriousness. He couldn't quite put his finger on it, but he sensed a distance, a guardedness in her eyes that hadn't been there before. He loved her, but this…this uncertainty was unsettling.

Meanwhile, miles away, in a cramped nondescript basement of their safe house, Big D, Tina, and Angela were reaching their breaking point. The initial thrill of their escape had worn off, replaced by a gnawing sense of confinement.

They were prisoners in their own gilded cage, cut off from the world, their only connection to the outside through a small webcam exchange setup that allowed them to glimpse into Jax's home and communicate when necessary.

"Another day, another four walls," Big D grumbled, pacing the length of the small living room. "I can't believe this shit."

Tina sighed, flipping through a dog-eared magazine. "Tell me about it. I haven't seen the sun in weeks. I'm starting to look like a mushroom."

Angela, ever the optimist, tried to lighten the mood. "I mean it could be worse. We have each other, right? We're family."

They missed the simple things, the everyday routines that they'd once taken for granted. They missed the freedom to walk outside without looking over their shoulders, the freedom to just be. The webcam became their lifeline, a window into a world they no longer inhabited. They'd watch Jax and Ke' struggle to go about their lives, an ever present reminder of all the damage sustained.

One afternoon, as they were watching an episode of Jax's house, they saw Ke' enter the kitchen. She looked pale, her movements hesitant. She walked over to the sink and gripped the edge, her knuckles white. Then, she doubled over, her body convulsing. She threw up violently, her shoulders shaking.

Big D, Tina, and Angela exchanged worried glances. "What's wrong with her?" Tina asked, her voice filled with concern.

"I don't know," Big D said, his brow furrowed. "She looks…sick."

Angela's eyes widened. "Oh my god," she whispered. "Do you think…?"

The thought hung in the air, unspoken but understood.

Back at Jax's house, Ke' leaned against the sink, her breath coming in ragged gasps. She felt dizzy, nauseous. She knew what it meant. The missed periods, the morning sickness…it all pointed to one thing. She was pregnant!

A wave of panic washed over her. How could this happen? Not now, not with everything that was going on. She wasn't ready for a kid. In fact, she never had the thought of having her own yet. She was young, living life developing into real womanhood and making her way, still trying to recover from traumatic events that now reshaped her life. She thought of Terry, his face and possible reaction and she thought of the future. Ke' knew she had to tell Jax, but the words wouldn't come so easy. The father of her child was a friend and associate of his that he had no clue about. Had zero knowledge of any relationship at all, and there had been plenty of time to mention it but never once had she. This could possibly create some unwanted friction. The last thing either of them needed.

She was trapped, caught in a web of lies and deceit, and she didn't know how to escape or hide. The truth about this would come out. Unbeknownst to Ke' this was all part of Terry's plan. But what that plan entailed, she couldn't even fathom.

Chapter 25
Odessa

The drive from Lubbock to Odessa was a blur of West Texas landscape. Flat plains stretching out to the horizon, punctuated by oil derricks pumping rhythmically, a stark contrast to the turmoil churning within Jax. He gripped the steering wheel tight, his mind replaying the conversations with Gabrielle. She'd been insistent. "Jax, you need to do this. You need to talk to him. Answers don't just appear out of thin air. Sometimes, you have to go looking for them, even if it means facing uncomfortable truths, and if you just can't face those truths you have to be willing to accept that and press forward." And she was right. He needed answers, about his father, about his family, about everything that had turned his life upside down. He needed to understand.

He knew his father, Marcellus, lived somewhere on the south side of Odessa. That's all his mother's testimony had provided. South side Odessa. The words echoed in his mind. As he crossed the city limits, a sense of ease settled over him.

This part of town…it felt familiar, too familiar. It resembled the East Side of Lubbock, the side of town that had shaped him, the side of town he'd fought to escape. Dilapidated buildings, cracked pavement, a palpable sense of struggle in the air. He had no address, no specific directions, just a name and a general location. And his father's face, etched in his memory from the few faded photographs his mother had kept. He found them as time

131

passed after her death while he and Ke' cleaned her house and went through her belongings. Those two going in the bedrooms of their deceased loved ones was one of the hardest things they faced in the recent months. Being surrounded by all their things and the scent and the presence hurt so bad because in reality they were no more.

Jax pulled into a small, run-down gas station just off Snyder Avenue, needing a break from the long drive and a moment to gather his thoughts. He went inside, grabbing a couple of bottles of water and some snacks. As he stood at the counter, waiting to pay, the clerk, a middle-aged woman with tired eyes and a name tag that read "ReeRee," looked him up and down. Her gaze lingered on his face for a moment longer than usual.

"Baby, what's yo name?" She asked, her voice blunt, unfiltered.

Jax was taken aback for a second. He wasn't used to such directness. He assessed the woman, deciding she meant no harm. "Jax," he replied.

"Boy is yo daddy named Marcellus?" She asked, without missing a beat.

Jax's breath hitched. He wasn't expecting this. "Yes," he said, a hint of surprise in his voice. "That's my father."

ReeRee's eyes widened. "Oh my god, for real? You talking about fine ass Marcellus, the one that got all them kids and stay down there in the apartments right up the street?"

Jax just smiled and nodded, a mix of amusement and disbelief swirling inside him. This was…unexpected.

ReeRee shook her head, a grin spreading across her face. "That's crazy. Y'all could be twins! He sho' did good with all y'all honey, yes lawd," she exclaimed as Jax paid for his items. "Tell him ReeRee said hey," she added as he turned to leave.

Jax walked out of the store, armed with more information than he'd had just minutes before. He couldn't believe how easily it had come. Had it not been for her unknowingly giving him the exact location, he probably would have just drove around aimlessly for a while, eventually grow frustrated and give up.

He got back in his car and drove down the street, following ReeRee's directions. He found the apartments, a sprawling complex of weathered brick buildings, their paint peeling, their windows grimy. He parked the car and took a deep breath, steeling himself for what was to come. He had no idea what to expect, but he knew one thing, his life was about to change, one way or another.

Getting out of the vehicle, Jax took in his surroundings. The apartment complex was a hive of activity and very diverse. People were out and about. Niggas doing what niggas do, while the women watched them do it and kids running around playing. Music blared from somewhere in the distance, a mix of rap and Tejano. The air was thick with the smell of barbecue and smoke.

It was chaotic, vibrant, alive.

He still had no idea which apartment was his father's, so he started walking, hoping something would click, some familiar detail would catch his eye.

As he wandered through the complex, two small children came running towards him. He glanced behind them, thinking they might be chasing after someone, but there was no one there. They were headed straight for him. The little girl, slightly faster than the boy, reached him first. She jumped up, wrapping her arms around his legs in a tight hug. "Hi Shax!" She screeched. The little boy, just a second behind, joined in the embrace.

Jax was completely bewildered. He had no idea what was going on. He hugged the children back instinctively, then gently disentangled himself. He knelt down to their level. "Hey there," he said, smiling. "My name's Jax, not Shax."

The little girl giggled. "Yes, Shax!" She insisted.

The little boy nodded vigorously. "Yo name is Shax! And you our brother!" he exclaimed, then giggled and punched Jax playfully in the leg. Jax chuckled, still confused but strangely touched by their enthusiasm. He looked from one child to the other, trying to make sense of the situation. He had a feeling this was going to be a long day.

Jax leaned down and asked the kids which apartment their daddy stayed in. The little girl pointed to one across the small courtyard, "That one over there!" she exclaimed. The little boy, bouncing on the balls of his feet, added, "And he's inside!" The kids giggle. "We love you, Shax!" And ran off, their laughter echoing through the complex.

Jax walked up to the apartment, a faded green door with a chipped peephole.

He knocked, the sound sharp. After a second, he heard a deep voice from inside. "Come in, it's open."

Jax opened the door and stepped inside. He was immediately surprised. The interior of the apartment was much nicer than he would have expected from the outside. The initial room was filled with tasteful decor. One wall was covered with what Jax assumed were family photos – a multitude of children, beautiful black smiling faces, snapshots of birthdays, graduations, and holidays. Jax's attention was immediately drawn to the wall, and he gazed at the pictures in amazement, recognizing a few faces from his mother's old photo album. Then, his eyes landed on a picture of himself, a younger version, maybe ten years old, a gap-toothed grin on his face. He stared at it, a wave of emotion washing over him.

Snapping out of his trance, Jax looked around the front room, searching for the person who had spoken. "Uhm, hello?" he called out.

"In the back, gimme just a second," the voice replied. A few seconds passed as Jax waited, still looking around the room, taking in every detail. Then, as the voice spoke again, a figure rounded the corner into the front room. In that moment, Jax laid eyes on his father for the first time in twenty-eight years.

Marcellus was shocked and shook his head, a bittersweet mix of emotions swirling within him. Finally seeing his son face to face, alive in the flesh. Oh, how he'd yearned for this day, to finally be a part of Jax's life. But he knew it came with a price. He'd heard the news, like everyone else, about the situations in Lubbock, the deaths, the speculation. He knew Mecia had passed recently, and the circumstances surrounding her death, though shrouded in mystery, had weighed heavily on him. He'd coped with it, tried to move on, but seeing his son now, alive and standing before him, rehashed all those raw emotions. When Mecia had first died, and he hadn't heard from Jax, he'd assumed he never would. He knew the deal they'd made, the promise she'd extracted, that she would tell Jax about him in an event like this, before her passing and one day they could possibly know each other if he agreed to stay away until she said otherwise. It had been nearly three months, and still no word. He'd figured maybe Jax would never know.

Since that fateful day in Marcellus and Mecia's history, the day she'd been killed because of his actions, she'd been done with him. She'd made him vow to stay away from her and Jax, period. Under no circumstances was he to ever approach them, or there would be a problem. And Marcellus reluctantly had agreed. He'd given her his word.

The silence hung heavy in the air, thick with unspoken words and years of separation. Jax stood there, unsure of what to say, which direction to take the conversation. He'd come seeking answers and clarification about things between him and his mother, and a full understanding on why he had a life without him but now that he was face to face with his father, the words seemed to catch in his throat. He looked at Marcellus, searching for some clue, some hint of recognition, some sign of what to do next.

Marcellus broke the silence, a hint of a smile playing on his lips. "It's great to see you, son," he said, his voice warm and inviting. "You're pretty quiet, but I imagine we have lots to talk about, huh? Come in here to the kitchen with me and have a seat. Food's almost ready." He gestured towards a doorway leading deeper into the apartment.

Jax wasn't sure how to navigate this conversation. He didn't know what to say, what to expect. This was all so surreal. Marcellus, sensing his unease, took the lead. As they walked into the kitchen and sat down at a small table, he began to steer the conversation. "You want something to drink?" he asked, opening the refrigerator. While grabbing a couple of sodas, he began to speak, his voice filled with a mixture of regret and affection. "Look, Jax," he said, handing him a can.

"You are a grown man now. So I'ma get right to it. I'm so sorry. For everything. For how things turned out. I missed way too much. And though I don't ultimately agree with how me and your mother settled on things, I do accept the blame in it all and I want you to know I'm sorry, " He paused, his gaze meeting Jax's. "Your mother…she was an incredible woman." He cleared his throat. "Do you know everything?"

Jax nodded slowly, his eyes meeting Marcellus's. "Yes," he replied, the single word heavy with unspoken emotions.

Marcellus's eyes reflected a deep, palpable hurt. Some truths, Jax realized, were just too painful to revisit. Marcellus asked, "Do you…do you want to talk about it?"

Jax shook his head. "No," he said quietly. "I'd rather leave that part of the past alone," He paused, then added, "It…it wasn't easy, learning everything. But…I don't see the point in rehashing it. It won't change anything." He explained. "The reason I'm here is…well, I wanted to meet you. Get to know my family. I have Ke', and I love my sister, but…sometimes I feel alone. Like even after all the money I've made and how far I've come some days I feel like I got nothing. I lost my friends and family. And with everything that's happened recently..." He trailed off, the weight of the past few months pressing down on him. "Even though things have calmed down, the threat of...death still feels close. Especially after everything my friend Gabrielle and I have uncovered. I just...I wanted to meet you. Anyone else who's family. Just in case." His voice was low, sincere. "This isn't about picking at old wounds or pointing fingers. It's...it's for my heart. For my sanity." He looked at Marcellus, a flicker of understanding in his eyes. "I'm a father myself," he said, the words carrying a weight of their own. "My child...it's complicated. With someone I've always had issues with. So, I understand."

Father-Son dynamics...they aren't always simple. And sometimes, if a father isn't around, it isn't always his fault. Or by choice in every scenario."

A small sigh of relief escaped Marcellus's lungs. He was grateful that Jax was so level-headed, so understanding. He'd been prepared for anger, for accusations, for a complete rejection. This...this was unexpected, but welcome.

Jax pushed on, the underlying purpose of his visit still present in his mind. "So, with that being said," he began, his voice steady, "I'm here. And I want to know...what I've missed. Tell me about my family, who we are and what I come from."

The two men began to eat, Marcellus having quickly put together plates for them both. As they ate, the conversation flowed, albeit tentatively at first. Marcellus filled Jax in on the chronological milestones of his life, the paths he'd taken, the choices he'd made. He spoke of his struggles, his triumphs, the mundane details of a life lived without Jax, yet always with the thought of Jax in the back of his mind. And then, during a lull in the conversation, he revealed something that made Jax's heart ache and notice why he always had strange feelings of eyes on him at random times when he was young.

"You know," Marcellus began, his voice low, "I told your mother I'd stay away. And I did…in a way. But…I broke that promise all the time."

He gestured for Jax to follow him, and they walked back into the front room. Marcellus led him over to the picture wall, pointing out photos, some that Jax had already seen, others that he'd initially overlooked. Among the pictures of Jax, Jax realized there were photos he didn't recognize, photos that his mother hadn't possessed. They were taken from odd angles, sometimes from a distance.

Marcellus explained, "In the beginning I was never too far away, Jax. I watched you grow. I know it's not the same as being there, but…I always carried my love for you. I even spoke of you to my other children. They all know who you are."

"So that explained the two adorable rugrats I met outside before I came in," Jax said with a laugh.

"Yeah, that was Kennedy and Scott, the youngest of the bunch."

Mar pointed to a group photo of a smiling group of young people. "The older kids watched you play football back in high school. They were your biggest fans when you made it big in the entertainment industry in Lubbock," He swept his hand across the wall, a look of pride on his face. "You have a whole family of beautiful young faces who look up to you, Jax."

And as he took in what his father was saying, analyzing all the photos, the faces young and old, some now familiar, many not, Jax finally asked, a hint of disbelief in his voice, "Damn, pops, so how many kids do you have?"

Marcellus grinned, a touch of self-deprecation in his eyes, and let out a small chuckle. Sometimes, even saying the number aloud himself just sounded ridiculous. "Well, son," he said, "including yourself…Ten."

Jax responded, a wry smile on his face. "The Lord said be fruitful," he quipped, then let out a genuine laugh. "But damn, Pops that's crazy work."

Marcellus chuckled. "What can I say? The Lord truly did bless me."

Jax, still processing the sheer number, asked, "Wait...I'm the oldest?"

Marcellus nodded. "That's right, son. You're the oldest. By a year and change." He then proceeded to tell Jax about his siblings, painting a picture of each of their lives. "Tyreke," he began, "He's 27. The next oldest. Born and raised right here in Odessa. He was into sports growing up, did very well. But college didn't pan out the way he hoped. He found a good job out of town, at a casino, been there since he was 18. Turns out, he's really good with computers, cyber security. That led him into a field where he's been able to do pretty well financially and establish some connections."

"Then there's Eli," Marcellus continued, "He's 26. A social media influencer, party promoter. Been building his name and brand here in the city for the last couple of years, pretty successfully, I might add."

"Kavieon is 24," he said, a hint of pride in his voice. "He's a senior in college down in Georgia. GSU. Been a starter on the basketball team all four years. Biggest one of the bunch, too. Six-nine! If all goes well, he'll be declaring for the NBA draft next year."

"Jamarion is 22," Marcellus went on. "Art major. Recently transferred from UTPB to Texas Tech. Actually, staying on campus, in Lubbock, same as you."

"Kimmie is 21," he said, his voice softening. "She's a mother. Beautiful little girl. She just moved back to Texas. She's into cosmetology, pursuing a career in that field."

"The twins, Javan and Kyaja, are about to be 18," Marcellus explained.

"Graduating high school this year. And then there's Kennedy, she's about to go to middle school. And Scott, the baby boy, he's in fifth grade."

Jax listened, taking it all in, his mind reeling. "Damn, Pops," he finally said, shaking his head and letting out a laugh. "You weren't playing no games, huh? We got a starting five with subs off the bench!"

As Marcellus pointed out faces in the photos, the family tree began to take shape for Jax. "That's Eli, always the entertainer," Marcellus said, pointing to a picture of a young man hamming it up for the camera. "And there's Kavieon, look at him, already towering over everyone even back then." He chuckled. Jax absorbed the information, trying to match the names to the faces, the stories to the pictures. Then, he stopped at a photo of Marcellus in his younger days, standing with another man who looked strikingly similar to him.

"Who's this?" Jax asked pointing to an old photo of a man that looked like and aged progression photo of Jax and his father.

"Now that would be the man right there. That's a picture of my dad. Your grandfather, Michael Price." A solemn look passed. "I sure wish you would have got to meet him."

Jax smiled at the picture. A pang of love and respect for a relative he'd never known. "What about this man?" He asked, pointing at another photo.

Marcellus's expression shifted, a hint of something unreadable flickering in his eyes. "Oh, that's my brother," he said, his voice a little softer. "Half-brother, anyway. Same dad, different mom. His name is Andre. Haven't had contact with him in a long time. You know everybody does their own thing and everyone has their own problems. Andre definitely had and for all I know, he could still be in Lubbock. Things change, you know? So much has changed over time." He shrugged slightly. "But I do know he had three kids. Your cousins. Two boys and a girl, I think and I think the youngest were twins. That definitely runs in the family on my daddy side. I'm sure they're running around Lubbock somewhere—"

Before Marcellus could elaborate, the front door opened, and Tyreke stepped inside. He paused just inside the doorway, his eyes widening as he took in the scene before him. He looked from Marcellus to Jax, then back again. The resemblance was uncanny. It was like Marcellus had just kept having the same kid, over and over. It was amazing how strong their genes were. Tyreke was a younger version of both of them, a living testament to the family resemblance.

"Oh shit, wassup, big bro!" Tyreke stormed in, a wide grin splitting his face. He rushed towards Jax, pulling him into a tight hug. Jax was caught off guard by the sudden burst of energy, but the genuine love radiating from Tyreke was impossible to ignore. He was genuinely happy to see him, to finally meet his older brother, someone he'd always heard about, looked up to from afar. He'd never understood why their dad, or any of his siblings, weren't allowed to approach or contact Jax. But seeing him now, in person, was an overwhelming joy.

He unleashed his hug, the two men slapping hands in greeting. Tyreke launched straight into conversation, his words tumbling over each other in his excitement. "Man, bro, what's up!" He exclaimed. "This is crazy, man! How are you? It's so good to see you, you don't even know! We've talked about you and seen you on TV for years!" And I come home and find you in the living room," Tyreke continued, shaking his head in disbelief. "Just crazy. How long you been here?" He asked.

"About an hour or so," Jax replied. "Just made the drive up this morning. Lil two-hour trip, nothing to it."

"Okay, okay, that's wassup," Tyreke replied. "Shit, you staying for a while? If so, man, that's dope! We can definitely tap in and get lit this weekend.

Everybody would love to have you out with us, I'm telling you."

"Well, honestly," Jax replied, "I didn't know what to expect down here, so I didn't come prepared to stay. Plus, I do have to get back to my little sister, Ke'. So, I'ma head back out at some point today. But I mean, it's good to meet y'all and see the family. I'll definitely come back so we can build our bonds, you know?"

"Well, if that's the case..." Tyreke paused, turning to Marcellus. "Pops, you think you can run the system without me for the weekend? I just left from up there and got it all situated. All I had to do was update the new camera settings. Shouldn't be any issue from that standpoint."

"You know computers ain't my specialty," Marcellus replied, "But yeah, I'm sure I can handle it for a few days."

"Good," Tyreke said. "If you can do that, I'm going with Jax for the weekend. That is, if he'll have me," he added, looking at Jax for approval.

Jax considered the offer, his mind working quickly. He wouldn't mind at all having his brother tag along. It would be a chance for them to get to know each other, have some fun, and build a real connection. But at the same time, a part of him hesitated. He knew he had a lot going on, a lot of problems swirling around him, and he wouldn't want to drag anyone else into that mess, especially family.

He thought about Ke', about everything that had happened. But looking at Tyreke, it was like looking in a mirror. He already knew Tyreke was smart, capable. He had a hunch that his brother could take care of himself. His vibe wasn't one of trouble or a tough guy persona, but Jax was willing to bet he could hold his own. I mean, he was looking at a spitting image of himself, so why doubt that?

"Yeah, that would be cool," Jax said, a smile spreading across his face. "Shit, it's no problem at all. I've got plenty of room at my place. You and the family are welcome anytime."

Marcellus chimed in, "Maybe we can make that happen in a few months, this summer or something. Get all the kids together once school is out. Kavieon will be back to visit, and we can all finally spend some overdue quality time. Whether you come down here, or we all come there," Marcellus continued, "Either way, that's definitely something we have to do, Jax. You gotta know, we all love you. We're here for you. The past is the past, and we can't do anything about it. But what we can control is the future, what we do from this point on. This world is too small not to know who your family is."

Jax agreed, nodding his head. The three men continued to talk for a while longer, the conversation flowing easily now, the initial awkwardness having dissipated. Marcellus asked Tyreke if he wanted to eat, quickly making him a plate.

While Tyreke ate, Marcellus continued to talk to Jax, sharing words of wisdom and positive encouragement.

Jax cherished the conversation with his father. It was everything he'd hoped for and more. Before he and Tyreke said their goodbyes and hit the road back to Lubbock, Jax hugged Marcellus for the first time. It was a simple gesture, but it spoke volumes. Then, with a final round of handshakes and promises to stay in touch, Jax and Tyreke climbed into Jax's car and pulled away from the curb, heading back north.

***

The bathroom door creaked open, and Ke' stumbled out, her face pale and drawn. She leaned against the wall, her breath coming in ragged gasps. The morning sickness, or whatever it was, had been relentless lately. She felt drained, exhausted, and more than a little scared. As she stood there, trying to regain her composure, her phone rang. She hesitated, then picked it up.

"Hello?" she answered, her voice weak.

"Hey," Jax's voice came through the line, warm and reassuring. "I'm on my way back to town. Should be there within the hour."

"Okay," Ke' replied, keeping the conversation short. "Drive safe."

"Everything alright?" Jax asked, a hint of concern in his voice.

"Yeah, fine," Ke' said quickly, perhaps too quickly. "Just...tired."

"Alright," Jax said. "I'll see you soon."

"Okay," Ke' replied again. "Jax," she added, her voice a little more serious,

"There's...there's something I want to talk to you about when you get home."

"Okay," Jax said. "I'll be there soon." He hung up, a small frown creasing his brow. Ke's tone had been strange, almost...hesitant. He hoped everything was alright.

When Jax's car pulled onto his property, the long driveway winding through the sprawling estate, Tyreke's jaw dropped. He was awestruck by the sheer size and opulence of Jax's mansion. "Hell yeah, bro this shit hard!" he exclaimed, a wide grin spreading across his face. "Ooh, the fam gone hate I got to come first and they missing out on this!"

Tyreke continued his enthusiastic appraisal of Jax's property. "Man, this go crazy!" he exclaimed, craning his neck to take in the sprawling grounds.

"You got, like, a whole compound here! Pools, Basketball courts, I even saw what looked like a putting green back there. Damn, bro, you're living large! Wait till I tell Eli about this, he's gonna lose his mind. He's always talking about leveling up, this is like...level ten!" He let out a low whistle. "And the house itself look like a muhfuckin' palace! I can't wait to see the inside."

Then, as Jax pulled up to the garage, Tyreke really lost it. His eyes widened, his jaw dropped, and he let out a whoop of pure excitement. Lined up before him were Jax's collection of cars, a gleaming testament to his success. But it was one car in particular that caught his attention, a sleek, futuristic-looking machine that made his heart race. "Oh my god!" he yelled, pointing at the Bugatti Chiron.

"That's…Chiron! Nigga, you got a Bugatti? I've only seen pictures of this thing! This is…this is…I can't even!" He circled the car, his eyes drinking in every detail, every curve, every line. He ran a hand lightly over the smooth, polished surface. "This a bad bitch right here."

Just out of impulse and love, Jax, being the kind of man he was, replied to his brother, "Well, I worked hard, bro, and I'm glad you appreciate it all. No cap, shit still blows my mind too, having all this, knowing where I come from. Shit's crazy."

Tyreke nodded, agreeing with Jax as he continued to take in every detail of the Chiron. Jax saw how much his brother was into the car and decided to do something he'd do for anyone he loved. "Tell you what, lil bro," he said, a playful glint in his eye, "Since you rode back here with me, how about you take it with you when you head home?" He winked. "I think she'll be in good hands."

Soon they made it inside, and the unreal moment for Tyreke was just getting bigger and bigger as he took in his surroundings. The grandeur of the mansion's interior was even more impressive than he'd imagined. The double doors swung open, revealing a vast foyer with soaring ceilings and a gleaming marble floor. A grand staircase curved gracefully upwards, disappearing into the second floor.

Tyreke's eyes darted around, taking in the exquisite artwork adorning the walls, the plush, designer furniture, the intricate details of the handcrafted moldings.

"Man…" he breathed, trailing off in awe. "This is…this is something else."

Jax chuckled, a hint of pride in his voice. "Come on, let me show you around," he said, gesturing for Tyreke to follow. He led him through the various rooms, each one more impressive than the last. The living room, with its floor-to-ceiling windows overlooking the sprawling grounds, the state-of-the-art kitchen, the luxurious dining room with its massive mahogany table. He showed Tyreke the game room, complete with a pool table, a custom-built bar, and a wall-mounted big-screen TV. "We can catch some games in here later," Jax said.

Tyreke was speechless, simply nodding and absorbing it all. He trailed behind Jax like a kid in a candy store, his eyes wide with wonder. He ran his hands over the smooth surfaces of the furniture, admiring the craftsmanship, the attention to detail.

He couldn't believe this was his brother's house. It felt like something out of a movie.

Jax led him upstairs to the guest suite, a spacious and elegantly decorated room with its own private balcony. "This is where you'll be staying," he said. "Make yourself at home."

Tyreke walked out onto the balcony, taking in the panoramic view of the estate. "This is insane, Jax," he said, shaking his head in disbelief. "I still can't believe this is real."

"Get used to it," Jax said, clapping him on the shoulder. "You're family. This is your home too, now."

They went back downstairs, and Jax led Tyreke to the kitchen. "You hungry?" He asked. "I can whip something up."

"Nah, I'm good," Tyreke replied. "Still full from Pops' cooking. But…I could use a drink."

Jax grabbed a couple of beers from the fridge, and they sat down at the kitchen island. The conversation flowed easily between them now, the initial awkwardness gone. They talked about everything and nothing – music, sports, their childhoods, their father, their hopes for the future. They discovered they had a lot in common, despite their different upbringings. They laughed, they joked, they shared stories, the bond between them growing stronger with each passing moment.

As the evening wore on, Jax decided to take Tyreke on a tour of the grounds. They walked around the pool, the water shimmering under the moonlight. They strolled through the gardens, admiring the manicured landscaping. They even ventured down to the putting green, where Jax showed off his skills.

"You're good," Tyreke admitted, impressed.

"Thanks," Jax said. "I try."

They sat down on a bench overlooking the estate, the silence between them comfortable. The stars twinkled overhead, a million tiny lights illuminating the vast expanse of the night sky.

"You know," Tyreke said, breaking the silence, "I always wondered about you. About what you were like. We all did. Pops would tell us stories about you, show us pictures. We knew you were out there, but…it felt like you were a million miles away."

"I felt the same way," Jax replied, his voice low. "I knew I had a father out there, but…it felt like a missing piece of my life. Like I was always searching for something I couldn't quite find, even though I got all this."

"Well, you found it now," Tyreke said, clapping him on the back. "We're here, bro. All of us. We're family."

Jax smiled, a genuine, heartfelt smile. "Yeah," he said. "We are."

They sat there for a while longer, just enjoying the peace and quiet, the feeling of finally being connected, of finally being whole. The years of separation melted away, replaced by a sense of belonging, a sense of brotherhood. They were family, and that was all that mattered.

As they walked back to the house, Tyreke couldn't stop grinning. He still couldn't believe how his life had changed in just one day. He'd met his older brother, the brother he'd only known from stories and pictures. He'd seen his incredible house, driven his dream car. He'd been welcomed into the family with open arms. It was more than he could have ever hoped for. He knew this was just the beginning of a beautiful relationship, a bond that would last a lifetime. He couldn't wait to tell his other siblings all about it. They were going to be so jealous.

But more than that, they were going to be happy. They were finally a family, all of them, together.

***

Ke' had stepped out while Jax was on the road and wasn't there when he and Tyreke arrived. She got back about an hour later, and after a quick search of the house, she finally found them.

"Hey, brother," she said as she approached, a slightly strained smile on her face. "We need to talk." She paused, noticing Tyreke for the first time. "Oh, I didn't know you had company. It can wait until later."

Jax waved her concerns off. "No, it's okay," he said. "Sit down. I have someone I want you to meet." He gestured between them. "Tyreke, this is my baby sister, Ke'. Ke', this is Tyreke, my little brother. We just got a chance to meet earlier today when I met my father. Tyreke wanted to get to know each other better and decided to come stay with us for the weekend."

The two shook hands and offered polite smiles. "Nice to meet you," Ke' said. Then, she paused, a thoughtful expression on her face. "So, if this is your brother," she began, letting the question and its implication linger in the air, "That makes him my…"

The thought hung there, unspoken. Honestly, Jax and Tyreke paused to consider it too. Jax and Tyreke were half-siblings, sharing the same father. But Ke' and Jax were half-siblings through their mother. So, technically, there was no true blood link between Ke' and Tyreke. But in Black folks' rationale, in the shared experience of family and community, they were siblings as well.

They laughed and spoke freely for a while, catching up on each other's lives, the easy camaraderie of family filling the room. Then, Jax remembered Ke's earlier comment. "Oh yeah," he asked, turning to her, "What was it you wanted to talk about? Is everything okay?"

In that moment, Ke wanted to just blurt it out, tell him everything. But she couldn't. It wasn't embarrassment, and it wasn't even because Tyreke was there. It was something else, a deeper hesitation. She didn't want to add any more weight to Jax's already burdened shoulders. And there was something else, too. She'd never told him about T.J. About the connection they'd formed behind his back.

She didn't know how he'd react to the news, how he'd feel about her being with someone, especially after everything that had happened. So, she played it off, changing the subject with a casualness she didn't feel. It wasn't like he had any idea, and she wasn't even showing yet. In her mind, she had time. Time to figure out how to break the news, time to pray that it wouldn't ruin the fragile peace they were trying to rebuild.

So, she changed the subject, steering the conversation in a different direction. "Oh," she said, trying to sound casual, "Uhh, I just wanted to let you know ahead of time that I'll be out all night. I'm planning on staying with a friend tonight. Didn't want you to worry or anything. You weren't here when I first thought about it earlier, so yeah, just letting you know. Plus, looks like Tyreke's here to keep you company now, so y'all will be good," Ke' added, a small, tight smile on her face. Jax didn't think much of it. He simply agreed and nodded.

"Okay, well, I'll catch y'all boys later. Have a good night," Ke' said, offering a quick wave. She turned and left, a sense of unease settling in her stomach.

Leaving Jax's house, Ke' pulled out her phone and sent a text to Terry.

"Same place?" She typed.

The dots bubbled for a split second as he replied, "Same time."

"See you there," she replied.

Ke's fingers tapped impatiently on the steering wheel as she navigated the familiar streets. Her destination, a discreet hotel tucked away from the main thoroughfare, held an air of secrecy, a clandestine rendezvous she'd become accustomed to. Thoughts swirled in her mind, a mix of anticipation and apprehension. She parked in the hotel's dimly lit lot, the neon glow of the sign reflecting in the rain-streaked windows.

Inside, the lobby was quiet, almost deserted. She approached the front desk, the night clerk's eyes barely flickering as she requested a room. A few minutes later, she was inside, the door locked behind her. The sterile, impersonal atmosphere of the hotel room was a stark contrast to the warmth of Jax's mansion, a reminder of the double life she was leading.

She stepped into the bathroom, the sound of the shower a welcome distraction. The hot water washed away the day's tension, leaving her feeling refreshed, if not entirely at ease. Time slipped away as she lingered in the steam, lost in thought. Suddenly, she realized how much time had passed. Terry should have been here by now. A frown creased her brow as she grabbed her phone and dialed his number. "Hey," she said, her voice laced with a hint of concern, "I'm here. What's going on? It's taking a while."

Terry's voice, smooth and reassuring, flowed through the phone's speaker.

"Hey, baby," he said, the warmth in his tone immediately disarming her. "I was just

about to call you. How's my queen doing?" He launched into a barrage of questions, inquiring about her day, her mood, effectively interrupting her own inquiries. Then, with practiced ease, he switched the subject. "So," he asked, his voice laced with playful curiosity, "Did you tell him the news yet?" He was referring, of course, to her pregnancy, and their relationship, both of which she had yet to disclose to Jax.

"No," Ke' admitted, her voice low.

Unbeknownst to her, Terry had her on speakerphone. Tory, his twin sister listened intently to her response. It wasn't the answer Terry had hoped for, but it didn't truly matter. He planned to reveal everything soon enough.

"Well," Terry said, his tone shifting slightly, "I finally got a call back from Stephen. To get in the studio. Things have been a little shaky after everything started happening a few months back, and my deal kinda got sat on the back burner." He added, with a touch of calculated sincerity, "I understand what Jax was going through, and how all of it affected business, so I didn't worry about it for a while. But now, as time passes, I have my career opportunities to think about." He explained, "I'm booked for three hours and want to get as much done as I can. But I'll be there right after."

Ke' added, a hint of desperation creeping into her voice, "I mean, if things at the record company aren't what they should be, why don't you just go and talk to my brother yourself? I mean, y'all are cool already. And maybe somehow, you could work in our situation and explain yourself. He might handle it better coming straight from you. You could kill two birds with one stone," Ke' said, her voice laced with wishful thinking, trying to deflect responsibility while genuinely hoping to help him.

Terry responded with calculated calmness. "I'll think on it, baby," he said, his voice smooth and reassuring. "I'll get back to you after my session."

Ke' agreed, a sigh of relief escaping her lips. They hung up, and she tossed her phone onto the bedside table. Weariness washed over her, a deep, bone-tired exhaustion. She sank down onto the soft mattress, the plush pillows cradling her head. The events of the past, the emotional turmoil, the weight of her secret – it all pressed down on her, demanding rest. She closed her eyes, and drifted off into what she didn't know would be her last piece of peaceful sleep for a while.

***

The atmosphere in Terry's new apartment crackled with dark energy. Him and his twin sister exchanged a look of shared disappointment. Ke's answer, her admission that she hadn't told Jax about the pregnancy, hung heavy in the air. They both understood the intricate web of Terry's plan, a plan that had even Tory, privy to his machinations, reeling from its sheer audacity. She'd been floored when he'd revealed the full scope of his wicked genius, the depth of his calculated cruelty. If Jax knew about the pregnancy and was happy, he'd be vulnerable, thinking of a future, a legacy to protect. Then, when the inevitable happened, and Terry snatched his soul he would quickly realize he's failed to keep his word miserably.

Alternatively, if Jax was angry initially, the eventual reveal of Terry as the father would amplify his rage, fueling a destructive fire. It was sick, twisted thinking, a level of calculated malice that only Terry seemed capable of.

"Okay, so what? She ain't tell the nigga. Now what?" Tory asked, her voice sharp, as she watched Terry meticulously dress. He was clad entirely in black, the articles of clothing suggesting a night of clandestine activity.

He pulled a black shiesty mask over his head, the fabric obscuring his features. He looked at himself in the mirror, his eyes glinting with a cold, predatory light. "Doesn't stop a thing," he said, his voice muffled but clear. "Just wait 'til I tell him myself."

He didn't need the mask, really. It just went with the attire, the aura of menace he was cultivating. He planned to be

152

barefaced for this one, to look Jax directly in the eye, to savor the moment.

"I'm really happy this moment has finally come," Tory voiced, a hint of dark satisfaction in her tone, "But I hate the fact that you won't let me go with you."

Terry wasn't having any of it. "I know, sis," he said, his voice firm, "But you gotta trust me on this one. I got this. Plus, you ain't gonna miss a beat."

"How so?" She responded, her eyebrows raised. "Whatcha mean? I ain't Jesus. I can't be two places at one time. So, what you saying? You gonna let me go with you?"

"Hell no," Terry responded, a smirk playing on his lips. "But you can tap in with these. I bought them online a few days ago." He handed her a sleek, black eyeglass case.

"What's this?" Tory asked, opening the case.

"They're live-stream webcam glasses," Terry explained, his voice laced with a hint of sadistic glee. "I'm gonna wear them when I do the deed. You'll be able to see and hear all the action from my POV, like a movie, on the connected tablet or TV app. All you need to do now is relax, watch, and wait for me to get back so we can truly celebrate and go forward with the plans we have in life. Everything ahead of us will be brand new, all left behind will be burned to ruins," he emphasized as he buckled a small backpack and threw it over his shoulder. I'll wear the glasses from the moment I leave the house until I get back. You won't miss a thing, and you'll be able to make sure I'm safe from afar. I'm comfortable doing it this way, knowing you're safe now," he continued. "Worst-case scenario, if things don't go how I plan, at least you can see what's going on and have a head start on doing what you need to do." He paused, his eyes meeting hers. "But don't worry," he assured her again, a chilling calmness in his voice. "I got this."

TO BE CONTINUED IN…

Keep Reading For A Sneak Preview Of
HUB CITY MENACE 4: Immortal Gangstas

CHAPTER ONE
Revelations

The rhythmic thumping of the subwoofer vibrated through the floor of the mansion's media room, a low, pulsing bassline that accompanied the roar of the crowd on the massive screen. Patrick Mahomes, a Lubbock hometown hero and Texas Tech football legend danced in the pocket, evading a blitzing defender, and launched a laser downfield. Jax, leaning forward in his plush recliner, let out a whoop, the smoky haze of his joint curling around his head.

"Hell yeah, that's what I'm talkin' 'bout!" he yelled, slapping the armrest. "Mahomes ain't playin' no games tonight!"

The sensational aroma of pizza, sliders, and hot wings mingled with the pungent scent of marijuana, creating a comfortable, almost nostalgic atmosphere.

Jax reached for his phone, the screen lighting up with an incoming call. "Hmm" he muttered, recognizing Terry's number. He tapped the green icon, bringing the phone to his ear. "Yo, Terry, what's good?"

"Jax, my nigga! How you doin', fam? How's everything been?" Terry's voice was warm, almost overly so.

"I'm straight, man. Just chillin', watchin' the game," Jax replied, his eyes still fixed on the screen.

"That's what's up, that's what's up. Just wanted to check in, make sure you were good. You know, with everything that's been goin' on, I been thinkin' 'bout you." Terry paused.

"Yeah, man, I appreciate that," Jax said, taking a pull from his Backwood.

"Everything's been real rough, but shit I'm still here."

"I can imagine, bro. I can imagine. Look, I know you're probably busy, but I was wonderin' if maybe we could link up sometime soon. Catch up, you know? In person."

Jax thought on it for a second and saw no issues, suspected nothing. "Yeah, man, that sounds good. Why don't you come through here to the crib?"

"For real? Tonight?" Terry's voice perked up.

"Yeah, man, come on through. We can talk about everything. It has been a minute. And I been meaning to get with you just had a lot on my plate," Jax voiced.

"A'ight, a'ight, I feel that. Ain't no thang. I'll be there soon." Terry's voice held a strange mix of patience and urgency. "Peace, bro."

The line went dead. Jax stared at the phone, a knot tightening in his stomach.

Just then, the doorbell chimed, a sharp, intrusive sound that cut through the room.

Damn, that nigga got here fast, Jax thought, a flicker of surprise mixed with unease. He rose from his recliner, a sense of anticipation washing over him. He moved towards the door, his footsteps heavy.

He reached the door and took a deep breath, steeling himself for whatever lay on the other side. He turned the handle and pulled the door open. Standing on the porch, bathed in the soft glow of the porch light, were two figures: Tuck, his face a mask of his usual street-hardened stoicism, and beside him, Dillon DeCair, one of the most formidable lawyers in Texas, his sharp suit and even sharper eyes cutting through the night.

"Aye, my muthafuckin' nigga. Man, I'm so glad to see you, fam," Jax exclaimed, a surge of relief washing over him. He reached out and wrapped Tuck in a powerful G-Hug.

He released Tuck, then turned to Dillon DeCair, extending his hand. "Mr. DeCair, always a pleasure. Thank you for everything." He appreciated this man for the numerous times he'd saved him or one of his own from the confines of the tainted justice system.

Dillon DeCair shook Jax's hand firmly, his gaze steady. "Jax, it's good to see you. We managed to navigate the situation, as you can see." He gestured towards Tuck. "Technically, Tuck is free. All charges dropped. He's in no jeopardy of being bothered with this particular case again."

Jax let out a relieved sigh. "That's great news, man. I was worried like a muhfucka."

DeCair's expression turned serious. "However," he continued, his voice low, "getting off on a crime of this magnitude…it doesn't go unnoticed. It puts a target on his back. Especially if he chooses to remain in the city. There will be eyes on him, Jax. And not all of them will be friendly."

Tuck nodded, his face grim. "I know, DeCair. I ain't stupid."

"Just be cautious, Tuck," DeCair advised. "And Jax, I'd suggest you do the same. This situation has ripples."

Jax nodded, his mind racing. He knew DeCair was right. Getting Tuck off the hook was a victory, but it was also a declaration. And declarations had consequences.

"Come on in, man," Jax said, gesturing towards the living room. "Let's talk about this inside."

Tuck stepped into the mansion, finally taking a deep breath and exhaling, a wave of relief washing over him. He felt a sense of peace he thought would elude him forever. He was excited to be free, back on the outs, and around Jax, who had been through so much recently. He remembered when Jax gave him a leg up, and he planned to have Jax's back through whatever storms lay ahead.

"Man, I can't believe I'm out that bitch," Tuck said, his voice filled with a mixture of disbelief and gratitude. "I thought a nigga was done for. But that bombing…that shit was a miracle. Straight up divine intervention. On God." He shook his head, a look of awe on his face. "Destroyed the evidence room, and just like that… Without that evidence, they had nothin' on me."

Jax listened, his expression carefully neutral. He and Big D had orchestrated the bombing, but for entirely different reasons, tied to the complex web of their own struggles. He kept that knowledge to himself.

"I heard about everything that went down while I was locked up," Tuck continued, his eyes meeting Jax's. "Man, that shit crazy. I don't know what's all true and what ain't, but I want you to know…I'm ridin' with you, Jax. Whatever you need. Just say the word." He paused, a flicker of fierce loyalty in his eyes. "You been through a lot, bro. Lost a lot. But you ain't alone. I got your back, no matter what."

"My nigga!" Jax responded, a genuine smile spreading across his face. He reached out and they dapped up, a firm, brotherly handshake. "Appreciate that. Means a lot."

"No doubt."

"So, what's good, my nigga? You fresh out, now you're here. We got a lot of shit to do and catch up on, but we can get to it soon. But right now, what do you need?" Jax asked.

Tuck let out a weary sigh, his shoulders slumping slightly. "On the cool, man, I'm tired as a bitch," he admitted, a flicker of exhaustion in his eyes. "Really just wanna shower, throw some different clothes on, and get some rest. Start over tomorrow, get right."

Jax nodded, understanding. "I feel that, Tuck. You've been through the wringer.

This place is home, ain't nothin' changed. You know whatever you need is here, nigga. Do you," Jax stated with a wave of his hand. "You can kick it in the pool house if you need some more room," Jax added. "I got my lil' brother with me right now, put him in a room on the second floor for his stay for a few days. He cool. It's plenty of other rooms and shit you know that, but I understand if you need you a lil space from other folks for a lil bit, know what I mean?"

Tuck skipped over the pool house part, his attention zeroing in on the "Brother" part. He was confused. He knew Jax's family, and the only brother he had was Marcus, whose fate was known to the entire world. Greedy and D. Lee were like brothers too, but he knew their story, a blow that damn near crushed him when he heard about it. So, who was he referring to? 'Brother'?" he questioned, giving Jax a weary look.

Jax gave him a reassuring look and answered, explaining, "After my mother's passing, I learned about my biological father and decided to find and get to know him. Discovered I have a big family on my father's side, a few brothers close in age. Tyreke got with me this weekend to bond or what not, and it's just a surprise to see you in the flesh again too." Jax commented, "Lost a lot of family, but I'm gaining some too."

"Shit, that's wassup, man," Tuck replied. "What y'all boys got going on right now?"

"We just chillin', man, watching the game. You know, Pat Mahomes on that ass, and this nigga bucking the future GOAT," Jax capped.

Tuck replied comically, "Yeah, lil bro trippin'."

Jax said, "Shit, you wanna come up with us for a bit? Have a drink, we still got pizza and wings, all that. Know I keep that pressure too, shit wassup?"

Tuck thought about it for a second but respectfully declined, saying he was just gonna do him for the night. He would get with them in the morning and start the day off right. He gave Jax his appreciation, said he couldn't wait to meet Tyreke, and cracked an inside joke with Jax as he departed, asking him did him and his brother look alike?"

Jax responded, "I ain't even gon' lie, we kinda do, fam. Our genes strong then a muthafucka," with a laugh.

Tuck laughed even harder, saying, "Aw shit, that nigga look like evil John Legend too."

That laugh shared was good for their souls but would be shortly enjoyed.

***

Jax returned to the media room to find Tyreke still holding on to faith Josh Allen would pull off the victory in the game. And to Jax's surprise, it looked just as if he might win. But with only a few seconds left, Patrick Mahomes just displayed yet again his unbelievable talents to the world and somehow managed to pull off the win with just a few incredible plays incorporating the big name stars in red, white and yellow alongside him.

"See, that's that bullshit shit right there," Tyreke said, trying to cope with the loss and hurt of a passionate fan whose soul just got crushed by their opponents.

Jax didn't rub it in too much and just stated to Tyreke that he may not see it yet, but Pat was the GOAT and to never buck him. Despite what anyone said, riding with that man, the odds were in your favor for the win.

Playfully, Tyreke said he was disgusted, and that game made his stomach hurt. But really, it was from all the food he'd eaten all day, and them spicy hot wings truly did him no justice. He regretted some of his choices that day as his stomach began to bubble. He knew what time it was.

"Yeah, whatever nigga," Tyreke said, rising from his seat. "I don't like how that game turned out, and I'ma go leave my review in your bathroom. Gimme 'bout 35 to 45 minutes," he joked. "Bout to go up in here and see what that gold toilet hitting for."

Jax laughed more and told him, "Don't wear out your welcome in that muthafucka," as Tyreke disappeared down the hallway. "Spray is up under the cabinet!"

He shook his head, still chuckling at Tyreke's antics, and picked up the remote to lower the volume on the screen. The crowd still yelled and chanted in celebration of victory as confetti rained from above. He was reaching for his lighter to set fire to the blunt he picked up off his weed tray, and before he could strike the BIC and ignite, the doorbell chimed.

About The Author

J. White is a 30-year-old African American author from Texas. He successfully signed a publication deal with the reputable powerhouse Lock Down Publications in the summer of 2024 just a few months after his release from prison. He has released three amazing books to date with more on the way! He's currently hard at work on his next project.

If you are active on social media, follow him on
Facebook: @JaxWhite or JWhite Presents
Instagram: @jwhiteprsents
X: @JaxWhite429

DM him for information on how to get an autographed copy of one of his novels.

Book 3 Questionnaire

Chapter One Discussion Question:
In 'Press The Button,' Mecia's brother, BIG D, makes a shocking return and immediately confesses to a violent act. How does this chapter challenge our understanding of family, justice, and revenge? Discuss the moral complexities of BIG D's actions and Mecia's reaction to them. Does the chapter justify his actions, or does it serve as a cautionary tale about the consequences of violence?

Chapter Two Discussion Question:
In 'Shattered Peace,' the immediate aftermath of Kam's death is depicted with raw emotion and chaos. How does the author use sensory details (sight, sound, smell) to convey the devastation of the explosion and its impact on the characters? Discuss how the characters' reactions—Jax's grief, Mecia's despair, and BIG D's sudden departure—reveal their inner conflicts and motivations. What does this chapter suggest about the fragility of peace and the swiftness with which violence can shatter it?

Chapter Three Discussion Question:
In 'Just The Three Of Us,' Big D returns to find an unexpected alliance between Tina and Angela. How does this chapter explore the themes of unconventional relationships and power dynamics? Discuss the women's decision to form a bond rather than fight over Big D. What does their pact reveal about their characters and their understanding of loyalty and survival? How does Big D's reaction to this revelation contribute to the chapter's exploration of these themes?

Chapter Four Discussion Question:
In 'The Unknown,' Big D grapples with guilt and confusion as he learns of Leslie's death and the escalating violence. How does this chapter explore the theme of uncertainty in the face of chaos? Discuss Big D's internal conflict and his struggle to understand the motives behind the attacks. How does the revelation of his niece's death change the dynamics of the conversation with Tina and Angela? What does this chapter suggest about the limits of control and understanding in a world turned violent?

Chapter Five Discussion Question:
In 'Echoes Of Violence,' Detective Crockette's investigation brings him face-to-face with Jax, revealing a complex web of connections and hidden allegiances. How does this chapter explore the theme of moral ambiguity and the blurred lines between law enforcement and criminal activity? Discuss the significance of Crockette's tattoo and its impact on Jax's understanding of the situation. How does the chapter portray the tension between personal grief and professional duty? How does the detective use the threat of the Corona Cartel to manipulate Jax, and what does this reveal about the power dynamics at play?

Chapter Six Discussion Question:
In 'The Morning After,' the characters grapple with the emotional and physical aftermath of the previous night's violence. How does this chapter explore the theme of vulnerability amidst chaos? Discuss the contrasting settings of Big D's intimate moment with Tina and Angela versus Jax's solitary contemplation. How do these scenes contribute to the chapter's exploration of emotional and physical safety? How does the use of sensory details, like the 'sickly yellow eye' of the sun and the 'scent of burnt cannabis,' enhance the reader's understanding of the characters' mental

states? What does the chapter suggest about the characters' resilience and their ability to navigate a world that has become increasingly dangerous?

Chapter Seven Discussion Question:
    In 'Unfinished Business,' Jax meets with Big D, Tina, and Angela in an isolated location to discuss their next move against Sullivan. How does the setting of the abandoned fishing shack contribute to the chapter's atmosphere of secrecy and danger? Discuss the shifting dynamics between Jax, Big D, Tina, and Angela as they plan their revenge. How does the chapter explore the theme of unfinished business and the characters' desire for retribution? What does the revelation that Sullivan is still alive signify for the characters and the plot? How does the chapter balance the characters' personal grief with their determination to take action?

Chapter Eight Discussion Question:
    In 'The Seed of Doubt,' Jax and Big D clash over the plan to attack Sullivan's farmhouse. How does this chapter explore the theme of conflicting loyalties and the burden of responsibility? Discuss the tension between Jax's cautious approach and Big D's impulsive desire for revenge. How does Jax's decision to abstain from the plan reveal his character development? What does the chapter suggest about the nature of family and the sacrifices made in the name of protection? How does the setting contribute to the chapter's atmosphere of tension and unease?

Chapter Nine Discussion Question:
    In 'Up In Smoke,' Terry, Tory, and Bundle revel in the aftermath of their destructive actions, while Bundle grapples with the moral implications. How does this chapter explore the theme of moral decay and the seductive power of violence? Discuss the contrasting reactions of Terry and Tory versus Bundle. How does their celebration reveal their

differing motivations and values? How does the introduction of Bundle's personal circumstances (his mother's illness) add complexity to his character and his involvement in their criminal activities? What does this chapter suggest about the consequences of unchecked power and the potential for moral redemption?

Chapter Ten Discussion Question:
In 'Silent Traps,' the tension escalates as Big D, Tina, and Angela attempt to execute their plan, only to be thwarted by Sullivan's security measures and a chance encounter with law enforcement. How does this chapter explore the theme of unintended consequences and the fragility of even the most carefully laid plans? Discuss the role of surveillance and paranoia in the chapter, both in Sullivan's actions and the escalating situation with the police officer. How does Angela's unexpected action at the end of the chapter change the dynamics and raise the stakes? What does this chapter suggest about the characters' desperation and their willingness to resort to extreme measures?

Chapter Eleven Discussion Question:
In 'Mysterious Ways,' Tuck's perspective provides a glimpse into the harsh realities of prison life and the ripple effects of the external chaos. How does this chapter explore the themes of hope and redemption in the face of despair? Discuss the significance of Old Man Nick's cryptic message and its impact on Tuck's mindset. How does the chapter contrast the mundane routines of prison life with the larger events unfolding in the city? What does Tuck's internal monologue reveal about his character and his desire for a second chance? How does the chapter use the setting of the prison commissary to highlight the themes of power, survival, and the possibility of unexpected change?

Chapter Twelve Discussion Question:
In 'The Last Laugh,' Bundle reflects on his actions and the unexpected turn of events that led to his newfound wealth. How does this chapter explore the theme of ambition and the consequences of betrayal? Discuss Bundle's complex motivations, including his desire for revenge against Jax and his hope for a better future. How does the chapter portray the relationship between Bundle and Kenny, and how does it contribute to the overall narrative? What does Bundle's decision to withhold information about the twins reveal about his character? How does the chapter use the contrast between Bundle's past and his aspirations to highlight the theme of personal transformation?

Chapter Thirteen Discussion Question:
In 'Can't Catch a Break,' Jax faces another devastating blow as Mecia is hospitalized, revealing she has been poisoned. How does this chapter explore the theme of relentless adversity and the breaking point of human endurance? Discuss Jax's emotional state as he navigates the chaos and uncertainty surrounding his mother's condition. How does the revelation of the poisoning add a new layer of complexity to the ongoing conflict? What does Jax's inability to reach Big D signify in this moment of crisis? How does the chapter use the setting of the hospital waiting room to amplify the themes of vulnerability and helplessness?

Chapter Fourteen Discussion Question:
In 'Nowhere to Run,' Big D, Tina, and Angela find themselves fugitives after a deadly encounter with law enforcement. How does this chapter explore the theme of desperation and the consequences of impulsive actions? Discuss the dynamics between the characters as they grapple with their new reality and the media's portrayal of them. How does the setting of the desolate West Texas landscape contribute to the chapter's atmosphere of isolation and

vulnerability? What does Angela's suggestion of the abandoned farmhouse signify for their situation? How does the chapter use the tension and uncertainty of their flight to highlight the characters' resilience and their determination to survive?

Chapter Fifteen Discussion Question:

In 'The City of Angels and Demons,' Gabrielle Renee' uses her platform to shed light on the Cook family's plight and the city's descent into chaos. How does this chapter explore the role of media in shaping public perception and driving social change? Discuss Gabrielle's personal connection to the Cook family and how it influences her reporting. How does the chapter portray the city of Lubbock as a battleground between 'angels and demons'? What are the various theories and speculations circulating about the attacks on the Cook family, and how do they reflect the city's state of unrest? How does Gabrielle's call to action at the end of her broadcast reflect the power of journalism to inspire change?

Chapter Sixteen Discussion Question:

In 'The Shifting Sands,' Christo and Jax grapple with the unraveling situation in Lubbock and the changing dynamics of the Cartel. How does this chapter explore the themes of power, loyalty, and betrayal within a criminal organization? Discuss Christo's internal conflict and his struggle to maintain control amidst the growing chaos. How does the chapter portray the shifting power dynamics within the Cartel and the impact of these changes on Jax and Big D? How does Jax's reaction to Christo's ultimatum reveal his character and his evolving sense of loyalty? What does the chapter suggest about the nature of ambition and the consequences of unchecked power? How does the setting of Christo's secluded villa contrast with the chaos unfolding in Lubbock, and what does this contrast symbolize?

Chapter Seventeen Discussion Question:

In Chapter Seventeen, Jax confronts the simultaneous threats of losing his mother and the revelation of his father's identity. How does the chapter explore the theme of fractured families and the burden of hidden truths? Discuss the significance of Mecia's confession regarding Cori and Jr., and how it contributes to Jax's feelings of failure. How does the chapter use the setting of the hospital to amplify the emotional intensity of Mecia's revelations, and what does it suggest about the characters' resilience in the face of overwhelming grief?

Chapter Eighteen Discussion Question:

In 'Echoes of the Past,' Mecia reveals the identity of Jax's father and the circumstances surrounding their separation. How does this chapter explore the themes of legacy and the impact of past choices on the present? Discuss the significance of Mecia's request for Jax to find his father. How does the arrival of Detective Crockerette at the hospital contribute to the chapter's atmosphere of tension and suspicion? What does this chapter suggest about the complexities of family relationships and the burden of unspoken truths?

Chapter Nineteen Discussion Question:

In Chapter Nineteen, Jax endures a devastating funeral while Big D is forced to watch from a remote location. How does the chapter explore the theme of grief and the isolating nature of loss? Discuss the significance of the diverse crowd at the funeral and what it reveals about the impact of the victims' lives. How does Jax's internal monologue during the service reflect his evolving sense of responsibility and his determination to rebuild? How does the chapter contrast the public spectacle of the funeral with the private grief of Jax and Big D, and what does this contrast symbolize?

Chapter Twenty Discussion Question:

In Chapter Twenty, Jax grapples with the overwhelming grief and isolation that pervades his life after the devastating losses. How does the chapter explore the theme of resilience and the struggle to rebuild in the face of immense trauma? Discuss the significance of Ke's decision to return to school and what it symbolizes for both her and Jax. How does Jax's internal conflict regarding his father and his son contribute to the chapter's exploration of family and legacy? How does the chapter use the setting of the empty mansion to amplify the themes of loss and the struggle to find hope?

Chapter Twenty-One Discussion Question:

In Chapter Twenty-One, Ke' forms a seemingly innocent connection with TJ, while Jax struggles with his grief and isolation. How does this chapter explore the themes of vulnerability and the search for connection amidst trauma? Discuss the significance of Ke's growing trust in TJ and the potential dangers it presents. How does the chapter contrast Ke's budding relationship with Jax's emotional detachment, and what does this contrast symbolize? How does the chapter use the introduction of TJ to create a sense of suspense and uncertainty about Ke's future?

Chapter Twenty-Two Discussion Question:

In Chapter Twenty-Two, Jax encounters Gabrielle, who reveals potentially groundbreaking evidence about Marcus's case. How does this chapter explore the themes of unexpected alliances and the pursuit of truth amidst personal tragedy? Discuss the significance of Gabrielle's revelations regarding Marcus's alibi and Detective Sullivan's potential involvement. How does the chapter use the setting of the dimly lit bar to create an atmosphere of both intimacy and suspense? How does the chapter's flashback to the party scene contribute to our understanding of Jax and Gabrielle's connection, and what does it foreshadow about their potential future relationship?

Chapter Twenty-Three Discussion Question:
In Chapter Twenty-Three, Terry and Tory engage in a seemingly lighthearted pool game, but their conversation hints at a darker, more calculated plan. How does this chapter explore the themes of ambition and the consequences of unchecked greed? Discuss the significance of the twins' newfound lifestyle and how it contrasts with their previous circumstances. How does the chapter use the pool game as a metaphor for the twins' approach to their criminal activities, and what does it foreshadow about their future actions?

Chapter Twenty-Four Discussion Question:
In Chapter Twenty-Four, Jax delves deeper into uncovering the truth, while Ke' experiences a potential life-altering event. How does this chapter explore the themes of hidden truths and the consequences of isolation? Discuss the significance of Ke's potential pregnancy and how it adds to the existing tensions within the family. How does the chapter contrast the physical confinement of Big D, Tina, and Angela with the emotional confinement of Jax and Ke', and what does this contrast symbolize? How does the chapter use the growing sense of unease and uncertainty to build suspense and foreshadow future conflicts?

Chapter Twenty-Five Discussion Question:
In Chapter Twenty-Five, Jax travels to Odessa and unexpectedly meets his father, Marcellus, and learns about his extensive family. How does this chapter explore the themes of family, identity, and the search for belonging? Discuss the significance of Jax's interactions with ReeRee and the children, and how these encounters contribute to his understanding of his father's life. How does the revelation of Marcellus's large family and their diverse backgrounds

impact Jax's sense of self? How does the chapter use the introduction of Tyreke to illustrate the complexities of family relationships and the potential for reconciliation?

Lock Down Publications and Ca$h Presents
Assisted Publishing Packages

Due to an increase in the price of services we have increased our prices. The prices below reflect the price increase as of 11/1/24.

BASIC PACKAGE $699 Editing Cover Design Formatting	UPGRADED PACKAGE $1000 Typing Editing Cover Design Formatting Upload eBooks to Amazon Upload Paperback to Amazon
ADVANCE PACKAGE $1,400 Typing Editing (line editing/content) Cover Design Formatting Copyright Registration Proofreading Upload eBooks to Amazon Upload Paperback to Amazon	LDP SUPREME PACKAGE $1,700 Typing Editing (line editing/content) Cover Design Formatting Copyright Registration Proofreading Set up Amazon Account Upload eBooks to Amazon Upload Paperback to Amazon Advertise on LDP's Amazon and Facebook Page

***Other services available upon request.
Additional charges may apply

Lock Down Publications
P.O. Box 944
Stockbridge, GA 30281-9998
Phone: 470 303-9761
Email: lockdownpublications@gmail.com

Submission Guideline

Submit the first three chapters of your completed manuscript to ldpsubmissions@gmail.com. In the subject line add **Your Book's Title**. The manuscript must be in a Word Doc file and sent as an attachment. Document should be in Times New Roman, double spaced, and in size 12 font. Also, provide your synopsis and full contact information. If sending multiple submissions, they must each be in a separate email.

Have a story but no way to send it electronically? You can still submit to LDP/Ca$h Presents. Send in the first three chapters, written or typed, of your completed manuscript to:

LDP: Submissions Dept
P.O. Box 944
Stockbridge, GA 30281-9998

DO NOT send original manuscript. Must be a duplicate. Provide your synopsis and a cover letter containing your full contact information.

Thanks for considering LDP and Ca$h Presents.

NEW RELEASES

BLOODLINE OF A SAVAGE 1,2&3
THESE VICIOUS STREETS 1,2&3
RELENTLESS GOON
RELENTLESS GOON 2
BY PRINCE A. TAUHID

THE BUTTERFLY MAFIA 1-3
BY FUMIYA PAYNE

A THUG'S STREET PRINCESS 1,2&3
BY MEESHA

CITY OF SMOKE 1& 2
BY MOLOTTI

STEPPERS 1,2&3
THE REAL BADDIES OF CHI-RAQ
BY KING RIO

THE LANE 1&2
BY KEN-KEN SPENCE

THUG OF SPADES 1,2&3
LOVE IN THE TRENCHES 2
CORNER BOY CHRONICLES
BY COREY ROBINSON

TIL DEATH 3
BY ARYANNA

THE BIRTH OF A GANGSTER 4
BY DELMONT PLAYER

PRODUCT OF THE STREETS 1&2
BY DEMOND "MONEY" ANDERSON

NO TIME FOR ERROR
BY KEESE

MONEY HUNGRY DEMONS 1,2&3
BY TRANAY ADAMS

HUNGRY FOR MONEY 1&2
BY SLIMBOS

A THUGGISH PASSION
KILLAZ ON STANDBY 1&2
LAND OF DA HOOLIGANZ 1,2&3
FRESH OFF DA PORCH
BY IRA B.

COUNTDOWN OF A KILLA 1&2
GUNS DOWN, BOTTOMS UP 1&2
SEX, MURDA AND GOD
BY LO-LIFE

THE LEVEL UP 1&2
BY LUXURY KING

FO'EVA ROLLIN' 1&2
BY ASSA RAYMOND BAKER

HUB CITY MENACE 1&2
BY J. WHITE

KILLA CREW
DYING FOR LIKES
BY ARYANNA

IF YOU CROSS ME ONCE 6
ANGEL 5
By Anthony Fields

IMMA DIE BOUT MINE 5
By Aryanna

A THUGS STREET PRINCESS 3
EMBRACING THE LOVE OF A BOSS
By Meesha

PRODUCT OF THE STREETS 3
By Demond Money Anderson

STANDING ON HER BUSINESS
BY DG SANTANA

GET IT IN SLUGS 1&2
B. STALLS

CORNER BOYS 2
By Corey Robinson

THE MURDER QUEENS 6&7
By Michael Gallon

CITY OF SMOKE 3
By Molotti

CONFESSIONS OF A DOPEBOY
By Nicholas Lock

TENDER
BY KHUFU

THA TAKEOVER
By Keith Chandler

BETRAYAL OF A G 2
By Ray Vinci

CRIME BOSS 4
By Playa Ray

Coming Soon from Lock Down Publications/Ca$h Presents

RAN OFF ON THE PLUG 2 by **PAPER BOI RARI**
STREET REDEMPTION by **TONY DANIELS**
SAVAGE FAMILY EMPIRE by **PRINCE TAUHID**
BAD BITCHES WIT' GUNZ by **DIESEL**
THE SINGLE LADIES by **DIESEL**
COKE BY THE TRUCKLOAD by **DIESEL**
PROBLEM SOLVED by **DIESEL**
TIPPIN' THE SCALES by **DIESEL**
OPPS CRY TOO by **SAYNOMORE**
A GANGSTA'S KARMA by **FLAME**

AVAILABLE NOW

RESTRAINING ORDER 1 & 2
By **CA$H & Coffee**

LOVE KNOWS NO BOUNDARIES 1-3
By **Coffee**

RAISED AS A GOON I, II, III & IV
BRED BY THE SLUMS I, II, III
BLAST FOR ME I & II
ROTTEN TO THE CORE I II III
A BRONX TALE I, II, III
DUFFLE BAG CARTEL I II III IV V VI
HEARTLESS GOON I II III IV V
A SAVAGE DOPEBOY I II
DRUG LORDS I II III
CUTTHROAT MAFIA I II
KING OF THE TRENCHES
By **Ghost**

LAY IT DOWN I & II
LAST OF A DYING BREED I II
BLOOD STAINS OF A SHOTTA I & II III
By **Jamaica**

LOYAL TO THE GAME I II III
LIFE OF SIN I, II III
By **TJ & Jelissa**

IF LOVING HIM IS WRONG…I & II
LOVE ME EVEN WHEN IT HURTS I II III
By **Jelissa**

PUSH IT TO THE LIMIT
By **Bre' Hayes**

BLOODY COMMAS I & II
SKI MASK CARTEL I, II & III
KING OF NEW YORK I II, III IV V
RISE TO POWER I II III
COKE KINGS I II III IV V
BORN HEARTLESS I II III IV
KING OF THE TRAP I II
By **T.J. Edwards**

WHEN THE STREETS CLAP BACK I & II III
THE HEART OF A SAVAGE I II III IV
MONEY MAFIA I II
LOYAL TO THE SOIL I II III
By **Jibril Williams**

A DISTINGUISHED THUG STOLE MY HEART I - III
LOVE SHOULDN'T HURT I II III IV
RENEGADE BOYS 1-4
PAID IN KARMA 1-3
SAVAGE STORMS 1-3
AN UNFORESEEN LOVE 1-3
BABY, I'M WINTERTIME COLD 1-3
A THUG'S STREET PRINCESS 1&2
By **Meesha**

CUM FOR ME 1-8
An LDP Erotica Collaboration

BLOOD OF A BOSS 1-5
SHADOWS OF THE GAME
TRAP BASTARD
By **Askari**

A GANGSTER'S CODE 1-3
A GANGSTER'S SYN 1-3
THE SAVAGE LIFE 1-3
CHAINED TO THE STREETS 1-3
BLOOD ON THE MONEY 1-3
A GANGSTA'S PAIN 1-3
BEAUTIFUL LIES AND UGLY TRUTHS
CHURCH IN THESE STREETS
By **J-Blunt**

THE STREETS BLEED MURDER 1-3
THE HEART OF A GANGSTA 1-3
By **Jerry Jackson**

WHEN A GOOD GIRL GOES BAD
By **Adrienne**

THE COST OF LOYALTY 1-3
By **Kweli**

BRIDE OF A HUSTLA 1-3
THE FETTI GIRLS 1-3
CORRUPTED BY A GANGSTA 1-4
BLINDED BY HIS LOVE
THE PRICE YOU PAY FOR LOVE 1-3
DOPE GIRL MAGIC 1-3
By **Destiny Skai**

A KINGPIN'S AMBITION
A KINGPIN'S AMBITION II
I MURDER FOR THE DOUGH
By **Ambitious**

A DOPEBOY'S PRAYER
By **Eddie "Wolf" Lee**

TRUE SAVAGE 1-7
DOPE BOY MAGIC 1-3
MIDNIGHT CARTEL 1-3
CITY OF KINGZ 1&2
NIGHTMARE ON SILENT AVE
THE PLUG OF LIL MEXICO 1&2
CLASSIC CITY
By **Chris Green**

LOVE & CHASIN' PAPER
By **Qay Crockett**

THE KING CARTEL 1-3
By **Frank Gresham**

THESE NIGGAS AIN'T LOYAL 1-3
By **Nikki Tee**

GANGSTA SHYT 1-3
By **CATO**

THE ULTIMATE BETRAYAL
By **Phoenix**

BOSS'N UP 1-3
By **Royal Nicole**

I LOVE YOU TO DEATH
By **Destiny J**

BROOKLYN HUSTLAZ
By **Boogsy Morina**

GANGSTA CITY
By **Teddy Duke**

TO DIE IN VAIN
SINS OF A HUSTLA
By **ASAD**

I RIDE FOR MY HITTA
I STILL RIDE FOR MY HITTA
By **Misty Holt**

A GANGSTER'S REVENGE 1-4
THE BOSS MAN'S DAUGHTERS 1-5
A SAVAGE LOVE 1&2
BAE BELONGS TO ME 1&2
A HUSTLER'S DECEIT 1-3
WHAT BAD BITCHES DO 1-3
SOUL OF A MONSTER 1-3
KILL ZONE
A DOPE BOY'S QUEEN 1-3
TIL DEATH 1-3
IMMA DIE BOUT MINE 1-5
By **Aryanna**

BROOKLYN ON LOCK 1 & 2
By **Sonovia**

A DRUG KING AND HIS DIAMOND 1-3
A DOPEMAN'S RICHES
HER MAN, MINE'S TOO 1&2
CASH MONEY HO'S
THE WIFEY I USED TO BE 1&2
PRETTY GIRLS DO NASTY THINGS
By **Nicole Goosby**

THE STREETS ARE CALLING
By **Duquie Wilson**

LIPSTICK KILLAH 1-3
CRIME OF PASSION 1-3
FRIEND OR FOE 1-3
By **Mimi**

TRAPHOUSE KING 1-3
KINGPIN KILLAZ 1-3
STREET KINGS 1&2
PAID IN BLOOD 1&2
CARTEL KILLAZ 1-3
DOPE GODS 1&2
By **Hood Rich**

STEADY MOBBN' 1-3
THE STREETS STAINED MY SOUL 1-3
By **Marcellus Allen**

WHO SHOT YA 1-3
SON OF A DOPE FIEND 1-4
HEAVEN GOT A GHETTO 1&2
SKI MASK MONEY 1&2
By **Renta**

GORILLAZ IN THE BAY 1-4
TEARS OF A GANGSTA 1/&2
3X KRAZY 1&2
STRAIGHT BEAST MODE 1&2
By **DE'KARI**

TRIGGADALE 1-3
MURDA WAS THE CASE 1-3
By **Elijah R. Freeman**

MARRIED TO A BOSS 1-3
By **Destiny Skai & Chris Green**

SLAUGHTER GANG 1-3
RUTHLESS HEART 1-3
By **Willie Slaughter**

GOD BLESS THE TRAPPERS 1-3
THESE SCANDALOUS STREETS 1-3
FEAR MY GANGSTA 1-5
THESE STREETS DON'T LOVE NOBODY 1-2
BURY ME A G 1-5
A GANGSTA'S EMPIRE 1-4
THE DOPEMAN'S BODYGAURD 1&2
THE REALEST KILLAZ 1-3
THE LAST OF THE OGS 1-3
By **Tranay Adams**

KINGZ OF THE GAME 1-7
CRIME BOSS 1-4
By **Playa Ray**

FUK SHYT
By **Blakk Diamond**

DON'T F#CK WITH MY HEART 1&2
By **Linnea**

ADDICTED TO THE DRAMA 1-3
IN THE ARM OF HIS BOSS
By **Jamila**

LOYALTY AIN'T PROMISED 1&2
By **Keith Williams**

FOREVER GANGSTA 1&2
GLOCKS ON SATIN SHEETS 1&2
By **Adrian Dulan**

YAYO 1-4
A SHOOTER'S AMBITION 1&2
BRED IN THE GAME
By **S. Allen**

TRAP GOD 1-3
RICH $AVAGE 1-3
MONEY IN THE GRAVE 1-3
CARTEL MONEY
By **Martell Troublesome Bolden**

TOE TAGZ 1-4
LEVELS TO THIS SHYT 1&2
IT'S JUST ME AND YOU
By **Ah'Million**

KINGPIN DREAMS 1-3
RAN OFF ON DA PLUG
By **Paper Boi Rari**

THE STREETS MADE ME 1-3
By **Larry D. Wright**

CONFESSIONS OF A GANGSTA 1-4
CONFESSIONS OF A JACKBOY 1-3
CONFESSIONS OF A HITMAN
By **Nicholas Lock**

I'M NOTHING WITHOUT HIS LOVE
SINS OF A THUG
TO THE THUG I LOVED BEFORE
A GANGSTA SAVED XMAS
IN A HUSTLER I TRUST
By **Monet Dragun**

HUB CITY MENACE 3 | J. WHITE

QUIET MONEY 1-3
THUG LIFE 1-3
EXTENDED CLIP 1&2
A GANGSTA'S PARADISE
By **Trai'Quan**

CAUGHT UP IN THE LIFE 1-3
THE STREETS NEVER LET GO 1-3
By **Robert Baptiste**

NEW TO THE GAME 1-3
MONEY, MURDER & MEMORIES 1-3
By **Malik D. Rice**

THE LIFE OF A HOOD STAR
By **Ca$h & Rashia Wilson**

THE STREETS WILL NEVER CLOSE 1-4
By **K'ajji**

LIFE OF A SAVAGE 1-4
A GANGSTA'S QUR'AN 1-4
MURDA SEASON 1-3
GANGLAND CARTEL 1-3
CHI'RAQ GANGSTAS 1-4
KILLERS ON ELM STREET 1-3
JACK BOYZ N DA BRONX 1-3
A DOPEBOY'S DREAM 1-3
JACK BOYS VS DOPE BOYS 1-3
COKE GIRLZ
COKE BOYS
SOSA GANG 1&2
BRONX SAVAGES
BODYMORE KINGPINS
BLOOD OF A GOON
By **Romell Tukes**

CREAM 2-3
THE STREETS WILL TALK
By **Yolanda Moore**

CONCRETE KILLA 1-3
VICIOUS LOYALTY 1-3
By **Kingpen**

THE ULTIMATE SACRIFICE 1-6
KHADIFI
IF YOU CROSS ME ONCE 1-5
ANGEL 1-4
IN THE BLINK OF AN EYE
By **Anthony Fields**

NIGHTMARES OF A HUSTLA 1-3
BLOOD AND GAMES 1&2
By **King Dream**

HARD AND RUTHLESS 1&2
MOB TOWN 251
THE BILLIONAIRE BENTLEYS 1-3
REAL G'S MOVE IN SILENCE
By **Von Diesel**

MOB TIES 1-7
SOUL OF A HUSTLER, HEART OF A KILLER 1-3
GORILLAZ IN THE TRENCHES
By **SayNoMore**

BODYMORE MURDERLAND 1-3
THE BIRTH OF A GANGSTER 1-4
By **Delmont Player**

FOR THE LOVE OF A BOSS 1&2
By **C. D. Blue**

KILLA KOUNTY 1-5
By **Khufu**

MOBBED UP 1-4
THE BRICK MAN 1-5
THE COCAINE PRINCESS 1-10
STEPPERS 1-3
SUPER GREMLIN 1-4
By **King Rio**

MONEY GAME 1&2
By **Smoove Dolla**

A GANGSTA'S KARMA 1-4
By **FLAME**

KING OF THE TRENCHES 1-3
By **GHOST & TRANAY ADAMS**

QUEEN OF THE ZOO 1&2
By **Black Migo**

GRIMEY WAYS 1-3
BETRAYAL OF A G
By **Ray Vinci**

XMAS WITH AN ATL SHOOTER
By **Ca$h & Destiny Skai**

KING KILLA 1&2
By **Vincent "Vitto" Holloway**

BETRAYAL OF A THUG 1&2
By **Fre$h**

HUB CITY MENACE 3 | J. WHITE

THE MURDER QUEENS 1-6
By **Michael Gallon**

FOR THE LOVE OF BLOOD 1-4
By **Jamel Mitchell**

HOOD CONSIGLIERE 1&2
NO TIME FOR ERROR
By **Keese**

PROTÉGÉ OF A LEGEND 1&2
LOVE IN THE TRENCHES 1&2
By **Corey Robinson**

THE PLUG'S RUTHLESS DAUGHTER 1&2
By **Tony Daniels**

BORN IN THE GRAVE 1-3
CRIME PAYS 1&2
By **Self Made Tay**

MOAN IN MY MOUTH
By **XTASY**

TORN BETWEEN A GANGSTER AND A
GENTLEMAN
By **J-BLUNT & Miss Kim**

HERE TODAY GONE TOMORROW 1&2
By **Fly Rock**

PILLOW PRINCESS
By **S. Hawkins**

SANCTIFIED AND HORNY
by **XTASY**

WOMEN LIE MEN LIE 1-4
FIFTY SHADES OF SNOW 1-3
STACK BEFORE YOU SPLURGE
GIRLS FALL LIKE DOMINOES
NAÏVE TO THE STREETS
By **ROY MILLIGAN**

LOYALTY IS EVERYTHING 1-3
CITY OF SMOKE 1&2
By **Molotti**

THE BUTTERFLY MAFIA 1-4
SALUTE MY SAVAGERY 1&2
By **Fumiya Payne**

THE LANE 1&2
By **Ken-Ken Spence**

THE PUSSY TRAP 1-5
By **Nene Capri**

DIRTY DNA
By **Blaque**

BOOKS BY LDP'S CEO, CA$H

TRUST IN NO MAN
TRUST IN NO MAN 2
TRUST IN NO MAN 3
BONDED BY BLOOD
SHORTY GOT A THUG
THUGS CRY
THUGS CRY 2
THUGS CRY 3
TRUST NO BITCH
TRUST NO BITCH 2
TRUST NO BITCH 3
TIL MY CASKET DROPS
RESTRAINING ORDER
RESTRAINING ORDER 2
IN LOVE WITH A CONVICT
LIFE OF A HOOD STAR
XMAS WITH AN ATL SHOOTER

www.ingramcontent.com/pod-product-compliance
Lightning Source LLC
Chambersburg PA
CBHW071208260626
47162CB00004B/1220